LAURIE BOULDEN

HIDDEN GEMS

By Laurie Boulden

Copyright © 2019 by Laurie Boulden
Published by Forget Me Not Romances, an imprint of Winged Publications

Editor: Cynthia Hickey
Book Design by Forget Me Not Romances

All rights reserved. No part of this publication may be reproduced, stored in a retrieval system, or transmitted in any form or by any means—electronic, mechanical, photocopying, recording, or otherwise—without the prior written permission of the publisher. The only exception is brief quotations in printed reviews. Piracy is illegal. Thank you for respecting the hard work of this author.

This book is a work of fiction. Names, characters, Places, incidents, and dialogues are either products of the author's imagination or used fictitiously. Any resemblance to actual persons, living or dead, or events is coincidental. Scripture quotations from The Authorized (King James) Version.

Fiction and Literature: Inspirational
Christian Romantic Suspense

ISBN-13: 978-1-0881-6757-1

Chapter 1

A bluster of wind nearly ripped the door from Lizzie's hand as she pushed herself into the coffee shop. She pulled the door shut as the first large plops of rain fell. Huffing caused her red bangs to fall back in place. "That was close," she muttered as the few drops fell into a downpour.

Lights in round globes hung throughout the shop. A bar of dark wood took up the far side of the room. On the wall behind it, colorful chalk provided a menu. The place was mostly deserted for mid-afternoon. Lizzie weaved through tables to get close enough to read the menu.

A man sat on a stool. His mop of red hair drew her attention. Her color had come from a bottle. His looked to be the kind a person was born with. She stiffened her spine and turned her attention to the chalkboard. Male distractions usually led to trouble. Coffee. Mocha. Latte. Chai. Bubble tea. She forced herself to read the words, but from the corner of her eye, she noticed sadness or maybe loneliness. He stared at the mug between his hands with the edge of his lips down turned. She scooted closer.

"Are you drinking the coffee or tea?"

He blinked. "What?" His face wasn't handsome, but with blue eyes and squared jaw, Lizzie wouldn't ignore him.

"Tea or coffee?" she pointed as she asked.

"Tea."

The barrister walked to them. "It's a British blend from my family farm." He spoke with an accent. "It's good straight or creamed."

Lizzie smiled. "I'll have a cup, creamed please."

"Would you like to join me?" The strange man pulled out the stool beside him.

"Are you sure? You looked deep in thought a moment ago."

He shrugged. "I could use company."

She scooted onto the seat, keeping a comfortable distance between them. The barrister returned with Lizzie's drink topped with swirls of cream. She held her mug to the other customer. "Cheers."

He chuckled, his blue eyes softening, as he clanked his cup against hers. "Cheers. I'm Wes."

"Lizzie. Good to meet you."

The door opened with a bang as a soaked couple ran through, giggling. Wes jumped, face paling, before lifting his mug with a dry laugh. "Storms make me jumpy."

"Glad we aren't in it." Lizzie tucked her hair behind her ear as she chatted. "This is good." She took another drink. "What do you do, Mr. Wes?"

He hesitated a moment, and then his eyes brightened. "I work in the jewelry business."

"You sell?"

"No, I deal wholesale. Gems and stuff."

"Really?" She placed her elbow on the counter and leaned her head against her hand. "Your girlfriends must love you."

His throaty laugh made her spine tingle as the reddening of his cheeks touched her heart. "There are perks. How about you?"

"I've spent far too much of my time placing calls regarding things I don't care about. I decided to start my own business. I make pet accessories."

"Like stuffed toys for dogs?"

She chuckled. "No. Fancy collars, designer carriers, winter outfits. It's amazing what people buy for their beloved pets."

"How'd you get involved in something like that?"

"I spent a summer in Albuquerque, learned a lot about leather-working. I have some general designs and a few baubles to put on them."

"Ever think about using real gems?"

"Where would I get those? And who would pay for that?"

"Have you seen the way some people treat their pets?" His smile widened as he repeated her words. "I bet you'd have no problem selling high quality pieces."

"How would I set them? The studs I use now have a loop in the back to sew into the leather."

"I could show you how to make a silver setting. I work with jewelry, remember?"

She shrugged. "It sounds intriguing, but I'm not about to invite you to my apartment. Don't get me wrong, I like you so far, but that's a long way from taking you home."

"Tell you what." He held up a card from his inside

jacket pocket. “Here's my cell number.” Before handing it to Lizzie, he wrote something on the back. “And this address, this is a studio space. We can meet there, and I can show you how to mount gems and tie them into the leather.”

It was a crazy idea. This stranger, offering to help? She shouldn't agree, but the temptation ... how was she supposed to refuse? She accepted the card. The printed front had a few blue streaks. Wesley Granger. “It's a public studio?”

“Middle of downtown. We wouldn't even be the only people in the place.”

“Well.” She wanted to take him up on the offer. And she could tell he *knew* she wanted to. His eyes gleamed and a smile tugged the edge of his lips. “Alright, I'll do it.” Her heart beat faster at the prospect. “But I approve every step of the way. Anything I don't like and I'm out of there.”

“Understood. I have a sister of my own, so I hope she’s just as forthright.”

Their conversation continued, but Lizzie thought ahead. What would she do? If she could get a decent price on some jewels, how long before she could quit her day job and focus on creating sellable pieces?

~

The studio on Fourth Street had a brick exterior with a wide wooden door. Wes stood at the entry, glancing up and down the street. Lizzie tossed her shoulder length hair as she pulled the colorful bag hanging from her shoulder closer.

“Good morning.”

Wes gave a start and then grinned. “You made it.” He gave another glance at the street.

Lizzie looked as well. “Everything okay?”

“Good to go.” He opened the door. “I think you'll love this place.”

The smell of paint wafted through the air. Orange and red sofas filled the reception area. Wes bypassed the main desk, offering the young woman a wink and a double tap against the granite counter. A long hallway started through the double doors. Multiple rooms on either side opened into a variety of studios. Paints and colors littered the floor of one of the spaces. In another room, a metallic statue increased in height as the artist soldered a pipe at the top. Wes motioned her into a room with two tables against the walls. Sunlight streamed from the edges of a gray shade covering the only window in the space. A selection of pliers spread across the first table. An anvil with a chain of silver hanging from it stood in front of the workbench.

The other table held an array of tools Lizzie had never seen. There looked to be a laser, an eye glass of some sort, an overhead lamp, and a blue gem. She raised the sapphire near the lamp. Light glittered across its surface. “This is beautiful. What’s it made of?”

“You don't think it's real?”

She looked at him. “Real? Something like this would cost a fortune, wouldn't it?”

He took it from her. “A small fortune, but it’d be worth it.”

“How would you set something like that?”

He placed it in the palm of his hand and held it toward her. “What do you think? Earring? Ring?”

She took the gem and held it against her ear. “Too large?” Unless she wanted her earlobes to start hanging lower. She moved it to her finger. The sides hung over.

"See? Also too big."

"Are you sure?" He laughed. "I've seen pretty crazy rings being worn."

She placed the gem at the base of her throat. "What about a pendant necklace?"

He seemed to study the spot for a few moments and then nodded. "I think a pendant would look perfect."

Her insides warmed at his intense gaze, even as the voice of reason tried to make her take a step back.

"Come on." He grabbed her hand and pulled her to the work bench. She sat beside him. He opened a drawer and pulled a ball of wire. "Silver."

He plugged an iron-looking tool into the wall outlet and set it on a wood block. "That'll get hot, so be careful."

Lizzie watched as he cut pieces of silver and then heated them into a single unit. He pulled a second ball of wire from the desk. "Silver is a softer metal. We'll reinforce the integrity of the piece using steel." He snipped the thin wire and soon the casement for the jewel sat on the anvil. "Hand me the sapphire."

She dropped it into his open hand. The gem fit the setting perfectly. He heated the thin fingers that would hold the gem in place and then used a small hammer to secure the pendant together. He rubbed the finished piece with lamb's wool and wove a thin chain through the eyehole. He dangled the pendant in front of Lizzie.

"Wow." The simple holder wrapped around the gem cradled it without detracting from its beauty. "That's amazing. You're so talented."

He shrugged, his cheeks coloring. "When I want to be."

Lizzie stiffened as he wound his arms around her to

hook the chain. “I can't take this.”

“No worries.” He sat back with a grin and touched one finger to the necklace where it lay at the base of her throat. “It isn't real.”

Lizzie felt her heart beat faster. “But it's beautiful.”

“Trust me, the woman makes the necklace.”

She blushed, and turned her head, hoping for composure. She drew in a steady breath. “What about smaller pieces? I would love to make a dog collar. I can pay you for them.”

“Maybe at cost. I'll have to think about it.” He looked around the room. “Do you think the studio would work for you?”

“To make my pet jewelry?” She laughed. “Of course. This is a crafter's dream setup.”

“I don't mind sharing the space. I’m hardly ever here.” He glanced at the door and lowered his voice. “Just never let anyone know about it. I’ve got friends I don't think I could handle the razing I'm sure to get if they find out about this place.”

“No need to worry about that. Your friends won't hear a word from me.” The quiet voice telling her to leave and forget the entire offer warred against Lizzie’s desire to finally succeed at something.

“How about we meet up tomorrow? I've got a few things that might work for you. They won't be as pretty as this one,” He touched the necklace, “But I think you'll like them.”

“I would love to.”

They left the room. Lizzie watched as he locked the door and dropped the key in his pocket. The metal key ring jangled. Instead of returning to the front, he continued along the hallway. “Back entrance. The artists like to use it when they want to slip in and out at all hours."

"I never knew this place was here."

"The building belonged to an old lady with too much money and time on her hands. She divided the first floor into the studios and lived upstairs. Since she's gone, the upstairs' been opened into a gallery of sorts. I'll have to take you sometime." He held the door for her, and then they were in a small parking lot behind the building.

"You're sure about the necklace?" Lizzie looked up at him.

He nodded, shoving his hands into his pocket. He still checked the area around them. "I'm sure. It looks lovely on you. How does eleven tomorrow morning sound?"

"Doable." She held her hand to him. He wrapped both of his larger hands around hers.

"It's been a pleasure. I'll see you tomorrow." He led her to the alley that went to the front of the street. By the time she stood on the sidewalk, he was gone.

~

"It might not be comfortable for the dogs if the brackets go all the way through." Lizzie turned the leather collar over. The lighter-colored back side of the leather had a softer texture.

They laid the six-inch strip of leather across the table. Three metallic studs had already been fastened to it. Wes handed her two green chips. She placed them between the studs.

"You could tie them with thread."

She shook her head. "That would hide the jewels. Look how pretty they shine. What about a holder like a button? Something simple that can be sewn into the leather?"

"Hm." He lifted the first gem. "Yes, okay. I think I have an idea. Let me put this together while you look through that box." He pointed to a small case with a lock on the front. A tiny key stood in the hole. With a twist, she was able to lift the lid. The inside of the box had been lined with white velvet. But it was the sight of glittering jewels that took her breath away. An array of colors and sizes filled the bottom of the container. She ran her finger through them. There had to be close to two dozen at least.

"My goodness. Whoever makes these deserves a fortune. These are gorgeous."

"The purity of chemicals nowadays makes it possible." He spoke as he leaned over the table.

She tried to see over his shoulder, but his project was too small. She rubbed a blue gem between her fingers. "I could never afford this kind of quality." There was the nest egg, but was she ready for a leap?

"Think of it as an investment. You can charge a hundred dollars for this collar."

"A hundred? Who is going to afford that kind of luxury for their pet?"

He laughed. "Have you seen the little old ladies around here? They'll take one look at your products and be willing to pay that and more."

He moved his hand toward her. In the palm lay the small green chip. Now it was encased in a delicate silver holder. The hole at the top and bottom would allow her to attach it to the collar without disrupting the integrity of the piece. She pulled thick black thread from her bag. She used the other table while Wes continued to work on the second piece.

Once the green gems had been added to the collar, Lizzie attached the buckle. “Here, hold out your wrist.” *Should be about the size of a small dog's neck.* She wrapped the collar around him, buckled it together, and twisted it so the decorated part showed. It looked perfect.

During the week, they were able to make two dozen cat and dog collars.

“Why don't you take these around and find a place to sell them?”

“I still think we should include your name on the back as one of the artists. How will people know?”

“I didn't do it to be known. In fact, I'd rather not be known at all. Not that I mind helping you. I think this is a terrific idea.” He placed his hand on her shoulder. “How would you like to meet at Arties for dinner tonight?”

Lizzie nodded. Not a bad idea. Wes proved to be an enigma. At times playful and friendly, at other times silent and moody. Ever watchful, though in their hours at the studio, he had yet to explain why. “I'll be there around six?”

He nodded.

Chapter 2

Lizzie dressed with care, braiding part of her hair so the highlights twisted. Her red short-sleeve sweater didn't feel too heavy for the early October evening and Wes' necklace hung perfectly over the edge of the scooped neckline. The black skirt made her legs feel longer, and the slight heel of her sandals accentuated her muscled calves. She turned, evaluating herself in the mirror and pouted her lips. Not what she was going for. She laughed instead, and the image looked more like herself. The slight wave of her hair bounced as she turned away from the mirror. Good thing she had a black purse with a thin strap. Slightly more than casual but not evening wear. Her shoes clicked on the tile floor as she exited the house. Excitement caused flutters in her stomach.

Upon entering the restaurant, she heard a collection of laughs from the far right. With a start, she realized Wes rose from a table filled with other men and a few women. He hadn't said anything about friends. A chill swept down her back as she met a look from a slightly older man. His eyes narrowed, and then Wes stood between them. He placed an arm around her waist and leaned close to her ear.

"I am so sorry about this. I had no idea they wanted to get together tonight." He looked at her, and she swore fear flickered in his blue eyes. "You don't have to stay if you don't want to. I'll explain."

Lizzie straightened. She was not going to slink away like someone not worth introducing to friends. "I'll be fine. Really."

Wes breathed deeply, and she got the feeling he wasn't pleased with her answer. He touched the necklace. "Keep this under your sweater. Okay? It's important."

She nodded, tucking the pendent behind the fabric so only the thin silver chain could be seen.

He kept his arm around her waist and escorted her to the table. "Everyone, I'd like you to meet Lizzie. Lizzie," he paused for effect and waved his arm around the table, "this is everyone."

"Uh, hi."

Wes led her to a pair of empty seats. He sat beside the older man with cold eyes, and she ended up beside a younger woman hanging all over the arm of another man about Wes' age. After ordering a coke and fish-n-chips, Lizzie twisted her hands in her lap. Wes stretched his arm across the back of her chair. His warmth eased some of the confusing anxiety twisting her stomach. He fiddled with her hair. It was kind of cute. Lizzie leaned into him.

Blocking the view of the large man beside Wes helped her relax. Two other younger men had similar facial features with heavy brows and large noses. The women with them giggled.

Another gentleman joined the group as main entrees arrived. The well-dressed stranger paused as he caught sight of Lizzie. The moment passed quickly. Wes bumped her shoulder with his. “Smells good. I’ll share my steak if you share your fish.”

Lizzie checked his seared ribeye. “I can accept that offer.”

He cut a few pieces and slid them onto her plate. Lizzie gave him half a flank of battered white fish. “Do you like sauce with it?”

Wes raised a bottle of ketchup.

~

After the meal, Wes and the older man, John, stepped away from the table. Lizzie laid her napkin across her plate. “I think I'll visit the little girl's room.”

“Back there.” One of the girls pointed at the hallway behind the bar.

Lizzie stopped in front of the ladies’ room. Further down, a swinging door led to the storage rooms. The door at the end of the hallway swung slightly, but Lizzie didn't see anyone. Inside the bathroom, she checked her nose in the mirror, replaced her lipstick, and made a quick use of the toilet. Hands washed, she returned to the hallway. Voices rose from the other side of the far door. She inched closer.

“I don't care what you have to do, get that gem back.”

“We split it. I have every right to use my share however I want.” Wes sounded edgy and irritated.

“We aren't splitting it, you idiot. I have a buyer lined up. He will provide the cash payment for your service. Do you think I need a woman walking around with a ten-thousand-dollar jewel around her throat?"

"There's nothing to connect the gem to Philadelphia."

"She's a billboard. Where will people think it came from? Get it off her. I want an exact count, and nothing had better be missing."

"This isn't fair. I did what you wanted. Why can't you leave me alone?"

"You're in this with the rest of us. Get it from your girlfriend or I'll get it for you. Neither one of you will like my way of retrieving my property."

Lizzie pressed her hand against the pendant beneath her shirt. What had Wes done? Footsteps sounded, and she hurried away, trying to make the other side of the bar before they came through the door. Her heart thundered by the time she returned to the table. Wes didn't look much better as he sat beside her. She kept her eyes on her plate, not wanting to meet his or John's gaze.

Wes leaned in. "Ready to go?"

She nodded. She offered a quick smile around the table as her goodbye, skipping over the man at the end. She could feel his irritation, his eyes trailing her as Wes walked her to the front door.

"That did not go as I planned. I'm sorry."

She grimaced but remained silent beside him. Her mind whirled.

Wes grabbed her hand. "Look, forget them. Meet me at the studio tomorrow. It'll be fine."

"I don't know. I was checking with the stores in town tomorrow about carrying the collars and bags."

"After you're done." He squeezed her hand. "I need to talk with you."

"Okay. I'll give you a call when I'm heading that way." He stopped at her car and made sure she got in alright.

~

Lizzie's heart still pounded as she arrived home. She dug into the drawer of the table in the hallway. "Come on, where are you? I know you're here somewhere. Ah, yes." She held a business card in her hand. A number had been written on the back. She dialed the number, fingers shaking.

"May I help you?" An unfamiliar voice answered the phone. She flipped the card to the front.

"Um, yes. I need to speak with," she read the name. "Amber Littleton. Would you let her know it's an emergency and to call me back as soon as she can?"

"Amber Littleton? Are you sure?"

"Yes. Amber. Let her know, okay?"

"Your number?"

Lizzie rattled off her cell number. Kathryn should recognize it, although her undercover sister probably wouldn't respond. No, that wasn't fair. She'd provided the means. Just because Lizzie never had to contact her before, didn't mean this would go unnoticed. She hung up the phone and reached for the necklace. Ten-thousand dollars? How was that possible? She pulled it over her head, letting it dangle on the chain in front of her. Light glimmered on its surface as it gently spun. *How could I have thought this is a lab-created sapphire*? She chided herself, then glanced at the phone. Nothing. She put the necklace back around her neck.

Sitting on the couch with her hand a hair's breadth from the phone didn't calm her shakes. Lizzie crossed the room and pulled the basket of collars from the bottom of the closet. The glitters as she dumped them on the floor made her want to cry. Of course, they were real. Why would Wes have a cache of gems? She breathed shallow to fight nausea. What did it mean, Wes having beautiful jewels he willingly shared with a near stranger? He'd be crazy to give away stolen gems.

She went to the computer. The google screen came up when she opened the web browser. But what to type? Stolen jewelry? John had said something about Philadelphia even though Wes never mentioned any other location. She searched stolen jewelry in Philadelphia. A litany of results showed down the page. Now what? She clicked on images. The collection of fashion jewelry made her realize her mistake. Wes must have stolen gems or jewels, not jewelry already set. She tried again. Crown jewels were popular, but nothing in the results suggested a large heist. How many gems had she seen? At least two dozen small pieces. There might be more. She fingered the necklace. This had come from somewhere. What else could be hiding in the studio?

By midnight, Kathryn hadn't called, but Lizzie had a plan. Until her sister decided to respond, she would dig deeper. Perhaps there was more than one detective in the family.

~

Lizzie rubbed her hands against her jeans to calm her racing heart. She stood in the hallway of the studio. Wes searched a drawer beneath the window. She took a deep breath and pasted a smile on her lips. She could do this. "You're here already."

Wes turned with a weak grin. Dark circles beneath

his eyes gave his face a pallid tone. He rubbed fingers through hair already sticking up. "Did you have any luck?"

Lizzie tightened her fists hidden in her jean pockets. "Two places, the dog store downtown and Animal Lodge out to the west. I split the inventory between them." Could she be making a mistake? Would putting possibly stolen merchandise for sale be considered aiding and abetting? The prices on the collars were super-high. They were safe. She and Kathryn could retrieve them when the time came.

Wes shuffled across the floor. "I'm sorry about dinner last night. I didn't plan to have the others join us."

Memory caused the sour in her stomach to burn. "Were they friends or family? John didn't look happy to be there either."

"Stay away from him." Wes drew closer, his eyes serious. "I mean it. If you see him, try a different direction. He's not any good. Not for you, leastways."

She chuckled. "With friends like him, why have enemies?"

"Something like that." He fiddled with the tools on the worktable and then looked at her. "Have you ever been involved with someone and regretted it?"

Something dark tugged at her thoughts, but she refused to dwell on it. She shook her head. "No. I wish my sister would give a little more attention, but I've never suffered from lousy friends."

"Lucky you. Too bad we didn't meet before..." His voice faded away.

She tilted her head. "Before what?" If he wanted to confess, perhaps this would be the time. She stepped closer to him. “Are you in trouble? Can I help you somehow?”

His laugh didn't sound funny nor amused. “I know all about trouble. And I'm sorry I may have involved you.” He took her hand. “I like you, Lizzie. I really do. If things were different…” his hands fell to his sides.

Confusion made her head swim. Lizzie wanted to help him. She wanted to tell him what she'd overheard, but he would never show her the jewels or tell the truth. “I like you too, Wes.”

He hugged her, and she swore he looked as if he could cry. “I don't suppose I could convince you to skip town, huh?”

She pushed away with a frown. “I just got here.”

“What about family? A nice visit this time of year is always good.”

She took another step back. “What's going on? Something is wrong, Wes. I wish you would share it with me. Let me help you. I have no family except my sister, who doesn't want to be around me. I'm alone.”

“Don’t let anyone else hear you say that.” He rushed his words, a muscle in his jaw twitching. “As far as the world is concerned, you have huge brothers willing to protect you by any means. You need to be careful.”

She gripped the neckline of her sweater, voice soft. “Because of you?”

He nodded. “I wish… Well, doesn’t matter. I want you to have this place.” He dropped the key on the table next to her. “I've paid the lease for a year and the others don't know about it.”

“Then why not stay?”

“Because the more I come here, the sooner they'll

know. I'd rather think about you bent over the work bench creating beautiful things.”

“Don’t give up. You have talent, Wes. Check the shops with me tomorrow, at least to say hello. They should meet the real artist.”

“The fewer who know about me, the safer you'll all be.” He kissed her, and she felt the goodbye.

The unexpected move froze her for a moment, and he left the studio with her standing dumbfounded, fingers touching her parted lips. She squeezed her eyes shut to focus. Wes had gone, but she wasn't ready to give up. Not yet. She grabbed the key from the table. He had just reached the back door, pulling his jacket around his ears before pushing through the exit.

She followed, placing her boot so the door didn’t close all the way. He seemed like a turtle trying to disappear inside a shell as he went across the parking lot. She stepped away from the converted house once she knew he wouldn’t see her. When he got into his car, Lizzie paused until he reached the edge of the driveway. She raced to her car. He hadn’t gone far so she caught up, keeping a couple of cars between them. His car turned into an apartment complex as her cell phone rang.

“I’m sure you have a good reason for contacting me.” Kathryn didn't bother with greetings or niceties.

Lizzie bit back a sharp retort. She didn't need to begin this conversation with an argument. “I wouldn't have called you otherwise. I need to meet with you. Something important is happening and I need your help.”

“Meet where? I'm working, Lizzie. What exactly is it?”

Lizzie pulled up to the curb across the street and watched Wes park near the south end of the complex. "I can't talk over the phone. This is important. I'm being threatened."

"Threatened? Who? What did you do?"

"I didn't do anything. I can't explain on the phone." Lizzie looked at the entrance sign. "Meet me at Hutchins Apartments. In Dalton."

"Dalton? How am I supposed—?"

She heard her sister take a deep breath. She could see Kathryn in her mind. Her eyes would blaze even while trying to hide frustration. "Please Sis. I need you. Just this once, I promise."

There was a sigh. "The soonest I can get there is Tuesday morning."

"How early? Eight? I'll meet you in the parking lot. I'll look for your jeep. You still drive that monstrosity, don't you?"

"Yes. I still have Aunt Kay's jeep. Fine. Tuesday. 8:00 a.m. Hutchins Apartments parking lot. This better be worth it, Lizzie. I'm risking a lot to do this."

Relief caused a sob to catch in her throat. "I know, and I appreciate it."

"Stay out of trouble 'til then."

"Same to you." Though she knew she wouldn't. Kathryn's job was trouble with a capital T. Two days to keep things in check, then Kathryn could help them. Lizzie leaned over the steering wheel and caught sight of Wes walking up the exterior stairway and knocking on the door of the end unit. The door opened, but Lizzie couldn't see who stood there. He disappeared inside.

Chapter 3

Kathryn Brussels slipped through the dark hallway throbbing with music from the Jay-T Club. Remnants of smoke machine fog burned her eyes. She paused at the back entrance to the building. Nothing from within the building cautioned her from leaving. Outside was not much nicer than indoors. Though the northern states were welcoming winter, Miami remained tropical, clinging to warmth and humidity. She opened the door. Distinguishing voices from the blaring music took a moment. No one else lingered nearby, she surmised, and passed through the door, using her body to make closing it quiet. Overhead lights for the back street didn't work. She kept to the deeper shadows, across a cracked parking lot, over a street, then under the tracks of the metro. She paused again at the base of the stairs leading up to the train station.

She glanced back at the club, then at the skyscrapers that blocked views of the harbor. Months of undercover work risked because Lizzie had a problem. Kathryn almost turned back. If Lizzie were in serious trouble, she'd know, wouldn't she? They were twins. Before she could change her mind, she trotted up the stairs into the metro station.

A grimy man took a step in her direction, but Kathryn stared directly at him, hardening her gaze. He backed away. No one else approached as the train stopped. A few stragglers were scattered through the car. Most of them had their heads down, earbuds connecting them to their phones. Kathryn resisted the urge to warn them about keeping a keen attention on their surroundings rather than the blip of whatever it was they watched. Two stops brought her to Adrienne Arsht. The doors opened, and she counted to twenty, then stepped out before they swung closed. There was no one else on the platform. Still, she kept to the shadows as much as she could, going between the bus terminal shelters, and jogging across the street to the parking lot. A few vehicles remained, including her jeep.

The train moved away with a rumble. Nothing else in the area drew her attention. She crouched, reached a hand beneath a wheel well, and pulled out the box with her keys. A few seconds later, she was inside the vehicle, wrapped with the scent of coconut car freshener dangling from the broken rear-view mirror. Though she started the car and rolled forward, she didn't turn on headlights until reaching the exit to the street. Three hundred miles of darkness loomed before her. There was still no internal signal that Lizzie needed real help. With a sigh, she went anyway.

Hours later, Kathryn checked her scribbled note from the brief conversation of her sister with the apartment complex sign. Hutchins Apartments had the sort of look that discouraged college students or those who didn't have jobs while encouraging solid workers with not-so-hot salaries. It was two stories. The enclosed stairway kept residents dry. White picket in need of a fresh coat of paint braced the second-floor balcony. Clusters of bushes on the ground floor gave opportunity for someone to hide. A bad someone.

She thinned her lips as she assessed the area in the morning sun. People were leaving, probably for work, and she garnered a few uneasy looks. She didn't need to glance in the rear-view mirror of the jeep to know why. She hadn't had time to change since leaving Miami. She'd driven through the pre-dawn hours and arrived in time to watch the sun rise over the quaintly dull town. Noise from last night's club still rang her ears.

She moved her wrist to view the watch masked among the bangles. "Come on, Lizzie," she grumbled. "I don't have time to sit and twiddle my thumbs." The apartment complex settled, and still no sign of Lizzie. Kathryn picked up her phone. She tried Lizzie's number again. Same result, nothing. She scrolled through the few messages, found one with Lizzie's address, and frowned. The address differed from the apartment complex. Kathryn copied the address and checked with google maps. Lizzie lived downtown, a few miles away. Why ask to meet here? She glanced at the time. Two hours late. She toyed with one of the piercings in her eyebrow. There it was, the sense of dread. Enough waiting. She tossed the phone on the passenger seat, started the jeep, and listened for directions to Lizzie's house.

Nobody was home at the cute craftsman bungalow Lizzie rented. The uneasy feel in her gut tightened. Had

Lizzie really gotten herself into trouble? She pulled up a map to locate the police station.

Chapter 4

Sergeant Marshall Franklin felt dwarfed by the ancient metal desk Captain Breyer had been kind enough to clear before leaving for vacation. He pushed against its orange side, but the monster refused to scoot away from the wall. How could Breyer feel comfortable in an office with the blank wall hovering over his shoulder? Grunting in frustration, he exited his temporary office space. "You'd be the first to go." He frowned at the offending furniture and walked through the door into the central room. He skirted his usual desk and pushed a chair under the adjacent desk. The color of the walls still made his nose curl. A fresh coat of yellow had brightened the space last year, but the color looked more like a tobacco haze than sunny or cheerful. Bless Captain Breyer, but the color-blind boss shouldn't have picked the paint. Marshall sighed. Something else he'd change if he were to become captain.

"If we find a body…"

The impatient voice of the newest addition to the force captured his attention. Officer Luke Hayes had the wavy blond hair one expected from a surfer, not a big city cop from the northeast. The elderly woman sitting at his side might explain the frustration.

"I know what I saw, young man." Jackie Groves sat straighter, her lips tightening.

Marshall moved closer to them. "Officer Hayes means no disrespect, ma'am." He placed his hand on Jackie's shoulder, drawing her attention. Her eyes were clear, bright with excitement.

"I know what I saw. This young man needs to accept that fact and get to work."

"Yes, ma'am." He turned to Hayes. "Where did this happen?"

"Hutchins Apartments." He looked at the report. "Over on Second."

"Yes, I know where that is."

Hayes tapped the monitor. "The report got called last night and we sent a patrol."

Jackie pointed a finger at Hayes. "It was dark, you don't know what kind of evidence could be missed."

"I'll arrange another look at the scene, Jackie." Marshall assured her. Hayes frowned, but he would learn to placate members of the community when necessary.

"They need to find that poor woman. Getting shot like that." Jackie crossed herself. "It isn't right, Marshall. Not in our town, that's not what we're about."

"I agree."

"Sir?" Another officer interrupted. "I think we need you up front."

Marshall sighed. Tuesday mornings shouldn't be this busy.

He crossed the room and pushed through the only door on the far wall. The short hallway led to the front entry and waiting area of the police station. Large glass doors welcomed the community into the building. The metal detectors were required but never an issue. Plush seats lined a wall, and a large library-style reference desk took up the other half of the room. Brenda, the dispatcher for their small police team, sat to one side monitoring the local systems while shooting glances at the citizen standing in front of Officer Dennis Mills. The older man's hands fluttered, his cheeks were red, and his eyes skipped from place to place, landing on Marshall with relief. Marshall raised his brows, but Mills jerked his head toward the front. Marshall looked and had to wrestle with himself to keep his features calm.

The woman standing at the counter was not what he would call traditional. A metal ring hung from her nose. Her brows boasted more studs than a farm. Her purple braid contrasted sharply with the vivid red shirt drooping off her shoulder.

"I asked for the person in charge." Her hands moved to her hips above a wide leather belt with silver holes. She smacked the piece of gum in her mouth. "I don't want to speak to another officer, I want someone who's going to do something." Her voice rose, complimenting the garish persona she emulated.

"Unless you want to wait for the Chief of Police to return from his fishing trip week after next, you've got me." Marshall stepped to the counter. Vivid blue eyes poured ice into his veins. What sort of vest could protect him from that?

She leaned closer, and Marshall fought the urge to

back away. "My sister is missing, and I don't appreciate sarcasm."

"Just trying to explain the situation, ma'am." He took a breath, waved Mills to the other side of the desk, and motioned for Brenda to turn around. He returned his attention to the woman. "What makes you think your sister is missing?"

"She called a few days ago to meet at the Hutchins Apartments parking lot. I waited two hours." She tapped her watch, "but she never showed."

"Plans change."

"Not hers." Those icy blue eyes narrowed, and he felt a chill across his neck. She continued. "And not mine. I took a risk contacting her."

"Why?"

Her deep-set eyes hooded when the main door swooshed open. He didn't recognize the person entering, but her body posture changed. She straightened, tossing her head back, making the ponytail sweep over her shoulder. The movement seemed like putting on an act. Curious. He motioned her around the desk. "Why don't we discuss this in my office? For privacy."

At her slight nod, Marshall pressed the release button for the swinging door. Her mini skirt and nets hid little from the imagination, and he worked to keep his eyes from her long, toned legs. The garish swirl of color he could see across her bra didn't help. With relief, he ushered her into his office and sat on the other side of the desk. The ancient metal monstrosity hid most of her from view. *I need to rethink that plan to upgrade*.

He cleared his throat. "I'm Sergeant Franklin."

She nodded. “I read the plaque on the door. Kathryn Brussels.” She reached inside her shirt, causing Marshall to hold his hand toward her in protest. With a sly grin, she dropped a small object on the desk.

The metallic clank of a shield made him frown. He lifted the silver disk warmed by her body heat. “Are you trying to tell me you’re a police officer?”

She crossed her arms and leaned back in the chair. “I’m not telling you anything.”

Her sarcastic response scraped across his patience. “Flinging that huge chip on your shoulder is not going to help us find your sister.” He slid the badge across the desk.

Her lips twitched and the hard edge of her gaze gentled. She slapped her hand on top of it.

“Are you undercover?”

Her pierced eyebrow lifted. “I don’t dress like this for fun.” She pressed her hand to her mouth, and he swore her eyes twinkled with mirth. “I’m sorry, it’s the persona. The mouth flaps right along with it. My name is Kathryn Brussels, and it’s my sister, Lizzie, who disappeared. She refused to speak with me over the phone.”

“And disappearing isn’t her MO?”

“Mine, yes. Not Lizzie’s.”

Marshall pulled a blank report form from the top drawer. “Leave me your contact information. I’ll have a look around and give you a call.”

“I’m going with you.”

“Not like that, you aren’t.” Her impossibly blue eyes chilled, but he refused to back down. “You’re what? Out of Miami?” With a nod from her, he continued. “This is a small town. Not only will you stick out like a sore thumb, most of our community members won't want to talk to you. If you're trying to find your sister, we might need to do that."

Humor warmed her eyes once more. "I'm not trendy?"

Not even close. He remained silent, hoping she would get the message. Her rolling eyes brought a smile to his face.

"Fine. I will adjust myself to the neighborhood." She stood, and Marshall quickly lifted his eyes to hers. She wiggled her brows, causing silver to shimmer. "I'll even dispense with the purple hair." She twisted her braid around one hand. "Although it's a pretty color."

He stood, clearing his throat. "Lovely. You said Hutchins Apartments?"

"Yes."

"Any idea why that location?"

She shook her head. "She has a rental house further into town. I think she knew someone at the apartments, but I don't know who."

"I'll meet you at the apartment parking lot in an hour."

She tossed her hair once more and walked from his office. He forced his eyes on a pile of notes stacked in one corner of the desk as she exited his office. No one deserved legs like that. Except maybe him. He groaned.

~

Kathryn kept her giggle inside. Why didn't they have leaders like that in her neck of the woods? At least he'd offered to help, even though her need to needle him couldn't have been in her favor. It must be the tall frame and wide shoulders. Green eyes didn't hurt, either. Marshall Franklin. Interesting.

She slid sunglasses onto her face but observed the station. One officer worked in the main room. The older man upfront filled in paper forms. Both wore khaki pants and blue dress shirts instead of the traditional uniform. The woman at the front wore a dress. It didn't seem like a harsh working environment. Officer Mills retained his position at the front desk. She couldn't resist a tiny wave in his direction as she sashayed through the glass door. His heightened color made her smile. She saw the dispatcher cover her mouth.

The downtown area had a splattering of people. She walked toward her jeep, aware of the stares and whispers following in her wake. An older woman glared and pulled her husband in another direction. She couldn't blame her. The hideous outfit belonged in a Halloween contest. She hid behind dark sunglasses, carefully monitoring the sleepy street while she crossed. Her beat up jeep waited beneath the oak trees. She brushed colorful leaves from the hood, glancing up and down the street. Nothing moved. She entered the vehicle. The engine roared to life with a slight turn of the key, and she careened from the lot. Nothing unusual posed itself, but she couldn't rid the niggling feel of eyes watching. Not the uncomfortable looks of normal shoppers, but someone sinister caused the unreachable spot on her back to itch.

Chapter 5

Marshall pulled his hand through wavy hair. He took a seat across from Jackie. "Did your son witness the attack?"

Jackie shook her head.

"He lives at Hutchins, doesn't he?"

This time she nodded. "Down on the corner. It's a lovely place. Such a delightful kitchen for cooking."

"I'm sure your son appreciates you." What were the chances Kathryn's sister and Jackie's victim being one and the same? He didn't like coincidence. "What time do you think you saw the attack?"

"Only a minute or two after ten. We were watching that show with dancing stars. My Beau and I, we used to do that." Her eyes faded.

He pressed his hand against her shoulder, drawing her back into the present. "I remember. Your son let you go to the parking lot alone?"

"It was late, Marshall, and he has to work in the morning. No one's going to bother a little old lady like myself. Not here, anyhow."

"Doesn't matter where you are, Jackie." He sighed. "You shouldn't traipse in the dark on your own. Let me head over and see what I see. Officer Hayes'll get you home."

"You're a good man," she said, patting his arm. "Find that girl. She deserves better."

He checked his watch. Enough time had passed. He didn't need Officer Kathryn investigating on her own. He wanted to slap himself for the derogatory thought. Undercover work was dangerous, and she'd been good enough to fool him. She deserved respect, even if he didn't want to give it.

~

Kathryn couldn't stop a wide smile as the dubious Sergeant Franklin gave her a once over and continued searching the parking lot for someone else. She pushed her hands into the back pockets of her jeans. "Guess I should feel flattered."

His attention jerked back to her, and she watched recognition spark. Interest sparked.

"Wow."

She could feel heat in her cheeks at his appreciative glance. "Nice compliment." She returned the sunglasses to her face. Nothing quite as good as an appreciative look from a man when you weren't revealing all God provided. He adjusted his jacket and she thought the soft leather looked good on him. She turned her attention to the parking lot. Stepping back into herself felt strange, that explained her off kilter response.

Another police vehicle pulled into the lot. "Reinforcements?" She joked, but his mouth frowned. He knew something. "What?"

"It isn't…there's a possibility…" His words seemed

to jump over themselves. He closed his eyes, drew a deep breath, and started over. She quickly slid her eyes from his chest to his face. "One of our more colorful residents made a report this morning. She claims she saw someone get shot last night."

"Lizzie." Levity drained away.

His hand touched her arm. A shiver coursed through her. He withdrew, and she rubbed both arms, chilled.

He shoved his hands in his pockets. "There's no body. A crew came late last night and found no trace of a crime."

"But you think she saw something?"

He shrugged. "I don't like coincidence."

"Where?"

He pointed at the end unit. "The witness came from there around ten p.m. She walked in the breezeway when she saw it happen. She ran back to her son's apartment to phone the police. Richard came down but found nothing. The officers came up empty handed as well."

"Bodies don't disappear."

"No, they don't." He agreed. "And Jackie isn't always in the present, if you know what I mean."

The reassurance did nothing to alleviate her concern. She knew. She knew in her heart something had happened to Lizzie. "Let's walk it out." He understood what she meant, falling into step with her. "How far into the parking lot?"

"Near the lights. That's how she could see them." He stopped and looked back at the stairwell. "She would have been there somewhere. Dark, so no one would have seen her, unless she cried out or they heard her run up the stairs."

Kathryn crouched, studying the asphalt. No cars sat beneath the light. Had there been any last night?

"What do you think?"

She was surprised he asked. "If someone had been shot, there would be blood splatter, traces that couldn't be cleaned up."

"We can try luminal. Jackie will have to pinpoint where she saw the shooting occur. We can't afford to spray the entire parking lot.

"We were supposed to meet this morning. Why did she show up last night?"

"How long did you wait for her?"

"Almost two hours. Then I wanted to drive by her house. She's not answering her cell. I came to the station when I saw her house was empty."

"She offered no reason for the meeting?"

She stood. "I'm not an easy person to get hold of while I'm working. I've been gone for months. No contact."

"Must be hard."

She shrugged. "Necessary. It's how I keep my family safe." Her stomach clenched. "At least I thought she was safe."

"Do you have any reason to suspect this is connected to the case you're working?"

"No, but what could she be involved with to get herself shot?"

"We don't know."

Kathryn turned away. "Let's get your lady friend."

"Jackie." He followed close on her heals and she could smell his musky aftershave. "She's a neighborhood fixture. She'd like your purple ponytail, probably try it herself."

Kathryn laughed, though her heart felt heavy. *Lizzie, where are you? What have you done and why?*

~

Marshall offered a hand to assist Jackie from the back seat.

She squeezed. "There's a lovely lady for you, dear. You didn't mention bringing a date."

Marshall's attention drifted to the other woman walking closer to the streetlamp. Sans the jewelry, not even any holes dotting her eyebrows, lips, or nose, and blue eyes more realistic—he felt drawn to her. Light hair curling around her face and her long legs were encased in jeans and the soft purple tee covered her shoulders. Jackie giggled and patted his arm. He shook his head to clear it. "No date, Jackie. She's helping with the investigation."

"More's the pity. Perhaps she can meet Richie when we finish. If he's home, I don't think that boy is where he should be."

Bad idea. "Let's start with where you were when you heard shots fired."

"Did I hear them?" She gave him a puzzled look. "Don't you think others would have noticed?"

"You didn't hear the gun?"

"No, Marshall. I saw the girl get shot. He must have had one of those quieting who-dickies."

He swallowed frustration and held the gate for Jackie to walk through. A path led to the archway where stairs rose to the second story of the apartment building. "No lights." He searched the short hedges. "They should have lights along this path. I'll bring it up with the super."

Jackie stopped beneath the arch and looked at the

lot. Marshall saw the light in the distance.

She gave a determined shake of her head. "Yes, I think this is it."

Marshall spoke into the walkie talkie. "Go to the lamp, Kathryn." A squeak of static responded, but he saw her move from the cars.

"No, she's too far. They were closer than that." Jackie closed her eyes, and then she nodded. "Definitely closer." She looked around. "More even with the palm over there."

Marshall looked in the direction she pointed and then barked more directions into the walkie talkie.

"Where's that other officer? Have him go stand by her."

"It's just us, Jackie."

"Well, give me this." She took the talkie from him and then shewed him away. "Go. I'll let you know when you have it right. They were facing each other, and he held his weapon low."

Marshall pressed his hands into his pockets while he crossed the black parking lot. Kathryn raised her eyebrows but remained silent. "She needs a recreation."

Static crackled. "Not so friendly, you two. You're supposed to be killing the poor girl."

Kathryn's eyes widened, and he could see her distress. He placed both hands on her shoulders. "We don't know anything for certain."

"No touching." More static from Jackie. "Back up a few feet. And move a little closer this way."

They obeyed.

"Now pull your gun on her."

"I'm not…"

Kathryn touched him. "It's okay." She withdrew

before Jackie could complain.

He held his gun.

"It was bigger. You don't have a bigger one, do you?"

Kathryn cracked a smile. "Is she serious?"

He grabbed the walkie talkie from Kathryn. "I don't have a bigger gun, Jackie."

"I do." Kathryn pulled a 9mm from beneath her shirt.

"You have a permit for that thing, right?" He holstered his own weapon and took hers.

"Oh, that's much better." Jackie sounded distracted, and he could tell Kathryn struggled not to laugh. "You'll have to tell me where to get one of those dear. They look very impressive."

"Last night, Jackie." Marshall interrupted. "What did you see?"

"There was a flash, and then she doubled over. You know dear, you look very much like that poor girl. It could be her standing there, same build and body type."

"Thank you, Jackie." Marshall returned Kathryn's gun and looked around. "We're close enough to the light to be seen."

"Did you bring luminal?"

"We'll have to wait until dark for the black light. Too much sun right now."

She grimaced. "I don't like waiting."

~

With the sun setting behind them, Marshall turned his spotlight to the area they wanted to search. Kathryn studied the dark surface, but nothing stood out. No stain, no globs of blood or flesh. He shook a spray bottle after handing her the black light. She connected the wires to the battery pack.

She studied the apartment building, waiting for him to finish his part. “You know, we’ve been here for hours, and no one has stepped out to talk with us.” Nicely groomed landscaping softened the complex. The brick had a red and white finish, traditional for the east coast. Well kept. A few doors had Halloween decorations or scarecrows hanging on them.

“Half the apartments aren’t rented. Lot’s still empty. Must not be many home, yet.” He began spraying. The swish of the nozzle blended with the sound of crickets and other insects hiding in the night. Moments later, asphalt glowed, confirming the presence of blood.

Kathryn felt her chest tighten. “Jackie witnessed something. Why the quick clean up? Who could have the resources to dispense with a body before the police arrived?”

“I want to see Richard. He was here while Jackie phoned the police. He had to have seen something.” Marshall studied the distance between the stairs and lamp post.

“What if it’s Lizzie?” Kathryn rubbed her abdomen, blinking moisture from her eyes.

“Hey. We don’t know.” He took her hands, rubbing softly with his thumbs. It felt like … caring.

What of her sister? “It’s a logical conclusion.”

“Not verified. Don’t give up hope.”

She didn’t want to. And with him standing beside her, the warmth of his hands encasing her own, she felt a reason to hope.

~

Marshall closed the crime scene folder with a sigh.

The investigation lacked evidence. Richard hadn't been seen. Blood traces offered no clues as to whose blood had been spilled. A jangling tune interrupted his thoughts. He pressed the speaker button.

"Someone's here."

The whispered words sent chills down his back. "Where?"

"Lizzie's. Someone's tearing up the living room, and I'm hanging in the bedroom closet."

A curse flew from his lips. "Of all the stupid … stay hidden." He stood, grabbed his keys, and reached for his cell. "I'm transferring you to my cell. If a patrol car is nearby, I'm sending them with sirens blaring."

He pushed buttons and switched on his cell phone before hanging up the land line. "Still there?" She made a sarcastic whisper. Marshall ran.

The police cruiser arrived before he did, although they both had flashing lights to break the dark. He noticed a curtain move in the house next door. Marshall clicked his mag light on. The front door to Elizabeth Brussel's house gaped open. Lights were on. He motioned for the other officer to stay near the front. With a tight grip on the flashlight and one hand on his holstered weapon, he edged around the side of the house and into the back garden. The mag light lit up shadows surrounding the bushes against the side of the house. No one lingered. The back garden was also devoid of persons.

"Whoever it was is gone."

Marshall jumped at the sound of Kathryn directly behind him. He swung around, and she shaded her eyes from the beam of light. He swallowed another curse. "What are you doing out here?"

"Lower the light. I'm going to be blind for a year." Kathryn grumbled.

He complied, and noticed her toes were painted a soft pink. "You shouldn't be out here in your bare feet."

"Thanks, dad."

"There could be glass. How did they get into the house?"

"It seems someone had a key."

Marshall swept the light once more across the garden. "I don't see a perp hanging out here. Let's get inside before the neighbors start coming out to ask questions."

"Turning police lights off will help."

They walked around to the front. Marshall directed the other officer to shut off the spinning lights from the vehicles. Peace settled over the street, but the itchy feel of being watched remained. It wasn't that much after midnight. Several neighbors might still be up. He gave a cursory glance at the houses he could see along both sides of the street. Nothing nabbed his attention, so he followed Kathryn into the house.

~

Kathryn watched Marshall pace from the drawers of the desk that had been tossed on the floor to the front window with its dangling blind. With a shake of her head, she tied her hair back in a scrunchie and righted a dining room chair.

Marshall stopped in front of her. "Of all the foolish … what possessed you?"

"What are you talking about?"

"Your sister's missing, and you search her house in the middle of the night?"

Hands on hips, she glared. "I'm planning to stay

here. I didn't expect someone to ransack the place. I don't exactly have anywhere else to stay in town." What gave him the right to rail on her? Her fingers tingled. Oh, she wanted to hit him, and hard. Who needed anger management? Anyone working with Sergeant Franklin.

"You should have said you needed a place to crash. We could set you up."

"I don't need to be set up. I'm an adult, in case you haven't noticed."

"Everybody's noticed. How could they not?"

After his bellowing voice bounced off the walls, he had the grace to blush.

Someone cleared their throat. "Foreplay's well and good, but I've got something interesting, if you care to look."

Another officer, Hayes, stood in the door and she felt her own face flush.

"Don't be ridiculous." Marshall swerved on his heel and exited the room.

Ridiculous, was she? He'd pay for that remark. She stalked after them.

"The sirens were a good plan. Perp took off before he found what he searched for." Hayes crouched beside a woven wood cabinet sitting in the living room. One door hung at an awkward angle from the bottom hinge. He pulled a rectangular silver canister from the shelf.

Kathryn's heart leapt. "That's Grandmother's. Her antique German tin. I didn't realize Lizzie had them." She bent beside Hayes. "Are the others down there?"

"Did your grandmother have this as well?" Hayes opened the lid revealing wrapped stacks of money.

Her mouth dropped.

Marshall gave her a cold glance. “Are there other tins?”

Hayes responded, though Kathryn kept a firm frown on her face in response to Marshall’s continued glare. “Two other tins, both empty.”

“How much in the first?”

“Ten, fifteen thousand.”

“Maybe Lizzie doesn’t like banks.” She scowled at Marshall. “Are the bills sequential?” She heard Hayes sigh, and realized they were doing it again, talking as though they were the only people in the room. “Are they sequential?” She asked, making sure to look at Hayes.

He flipped through a stack. “Don’t appear to be.”

“Check the numbers anyway. See if there’s a trace on them.” Marshall toned down his voice, but Kathryn felt the desire to stick her tongue out at him.

~

Embarrassment pulled at him. He followed Kathryn from the house to the cars parked along the street. Kathryn had done nothing to warrant his boorish behavior. He had a sinking suspicion if she’d been anyone else, he wouldn’t have behaved that way. He’d known her a day, and already she was under his skin. The investigation continued inside Lizzie’s house, but they were no longer necessary. Though too dark to see the chips of ice in her eyes, he could feel disdain rolling from her. “I’m sorry.” He faced her in the parking lot with a car standing between them. He took a deep breath. In for a dime … “I heard your situation, and I panicked. Not something I usually do. And then I took it out on you. Again, not something I tend to do.”

Anger blazed from every pore. “I’m an undercover

detective." Her quiet voice cut worse than if she screamed at him. "You think I haven't gotten myself through sticky situations? I called for backup, not rescue."

"Backup?" He pushed closer, his own ire rising. She could, at least, admit she needed help. "You were hiding in a closet."

"Because a maniac trashed the living area. Doesn't mean I didn't get a picture of him."

"You have a picture? You photograph the suspect and you're just telling me now?" He looked at his watch for effect.

"My sister is the one who's missing. I have skills to do the job. You and your crew aren't getting anywhere, someone has to."

"No one knows what your sister is involved with. Surely you understand the benefit of working with partners?"

"Sure. Just not you." With a grand huff, she turned and walk away. He let her go. Okay. He needed to let her walk away. She seriously disrupted his peace of mind. He rubbed his eyes. What happened to the apology he'd attempted?

~

Ill words coursed through her mind. How dare he? Of all the places her sister had to find trouble, why here? Where this man failed to grasp the realities of a female officer's life? She needed sleep and lots of coffee. Probably a sticky bun. And then when next they met, she wouldn't feel the need to plow her fist against his Roman nose. A giggle escaped. Someone already had, and it didn't surprise her in the least.

She sat on a rocker on the front porch waiting for

the CSI unit to finish inside the house. Several neighbors remained alert with front porch lights blazing and light spilling through curtains. She had her gun in a pouch on her lap. Not a guarantee against trouble, but it would make a difference.

Footsteps of the tall, thin deputy caused wood planks on the porch to squeak. Hayes cleared his throat. “We’re just about finished. Sure you want to spend the night? There’s a hotel in town.”

“I’ll be fine. Alarm code’ll be changed just in case and I’ll have my gun under the pillow.”

“You know that’s not a wise way to sleep?”

“Normally, I’d agree. If someone decides to come back tonight, they might regret it.”

“All the same, keep your cell closer. Call if something happens.”

Kathryn chuckled, then muttered, “I’m sure he’d love that.”

“What?”

“I’ll be sure to do that. Thank you. Are you taking the antique tin?”

“For now. We’ll keep the tin and money safe until we know what’s going on. Any other hiding places your sister might have used?”

“For what?”

“Something she might have been working on? What sort of projects was she involved in?”

Kathryn shrugged. “Honestly, I don’t know. I haven’t seen her in months. She moved here hoping to be closer. Work made that difficult.”

“Life of a cop, huh?”

Kathryn stood. “If ya’ll are finished, I’m going to get inside.”

Hayes nodded. “Stay safe. We’ll send a patrol car through the neighborhood every hour or so.”

Kathryn thanked him, entered the house, and closed the door. She pressed a few buttons on the security monitor, shaking her head. “You shouldn’t use the same password for everything, Sis.” With the alarm on and house lights off, Kathryn glanced through the long side window beside the door. Officer Hayes stood beside his car and gave the house a once-over before getting in and driving away. It was going to be a long night.

Chapter 6

Morning arrived too quickly for Marshall, even though he'd stumbled through most of the night unable to fall asleep. She remained on his mind, and she was his first thought when the alarm buzzed in his ear. Groaning, he struck the appropriate button and rolled over, anticipating a few more minutes. Instead, his phone disturbed him this time. With a sigh of regret, he stretched his hand to the nightstand and fumbled for the cell. His holstered revolver slid out of the way, and he achieved his goal.

"Franklin." He growled.

"Teens found a body behind 22nd Avenue." Hayes did not sound overly tired, even though he'd gotten less sleep than Marshall.

Marshall closed his eyes. They both knew the likely victim. "I can be there in twenty. Keep it quiet until we get an ID."

Before an hour passed, Marshall knelt beside the body, holding a thick handkerchief against his mouth and nose. Domed lights through the alley revealed the body. Empty boxes had been pushed to the side. Insects crawling across the ruddy cheek had his skin crawling. The victim was male. Relief washed through him. The unfortunate young man with red hair gazed sightlessly at the brick wall.

Marshall stood and brushed debris from his jeans. “Get the ME on the body. Let’s ID him. Find his connection to Lizzie Brussels.”

“Think it’s possible?” Hayes clicked the camera.

“I don’t like coincidence.”

“Right, boss.”

“Don’t do that when the chief gets back. I like my end parts.”

Hayes laughed.

Marshall checked the alley and the street. “Didn’t you say teens called it in?”

Hayes nodded.

“At this time of the morning? Here?”

Hayes looked down. “If you can understand the behavior of teens, you’re better off than the rest of us.”

“Who was it? I’d like to talk with them. We’ll need a report.”

“They didn’t leave names. Called it in anonymous.” Hayes stood. “Would you like me to photograph the rest of the alley?”

“Yes. I’m going to check the street.” Marshall walked toward 22nd Avenue, using his flashlight to search the cement. The sun had yet to do more than touch the sky with a fairer blue.

A body slammed into him. His breath caught. A shapely body smelling exactly like the woman who had the ability to knock his even temper to the curb. She pushed against him, and his arms wrapped around her. "Easy, Punk."

She tried to jerk away. "They said there's a body."

"It's not your sister. Older chap, not Lizzie."

The words registered, and the lump that had formed in her stomach magically disappeared. Then, she realized Marshall's arms encased her and her hands lay against his chest. She owed him. She balled his shirt in her hands, pulled him closer, and pressed her lips against his. He stiffened in surprise, and then his hands moved to her head, fingers splayed through her hair. He tilted his mouth, warming their kiss. Oh, what a kiss. She'd meant to tease him, irk him for his thoughtless words yesterday. Yesterday. The day they met. With a gasp, she pulled away, both a bit breathless.

"That sure beats coffee," he joked, but his hand lingered on her face.

"Probably not a good idea."

"What's not good? The sun's rising and I'm holding a beautiful woman in my arms."

"Uh, huh." She took a step back. "I was happy to hear my sister isn't lying dead in an alley."

"Come on. Let's grab a cup of coffee and find your sister." He took her elbow and led her to the street, heading north.

"No. I want to see the body first."

"I can't let you into a crime scene."

She pressed her hands against her hips. "I am a police officer. You can't know for sure if this has to do with Lizzie's disappearance or not."

"How is observing a body going to help? Or do you know more than you're telling?"

"I have the photo from the house last night. We can at least see if it's the same guy."

"Did you send a copy to our tech?"

"Did you give me a number to text?" Irritation tugged at her. Irritation explained the twisting in her gut. It *didn't* explain why she wanted to grin while standing nearly toe to toe with the man.

"You two done?" Hayes cleared his throat. Kathryn stepped back and Marshall turned around.

"Take her to see the body. She has a photo on her phone. Compare the two."

She followed the younger man. "I can guess why there are no female officers in this precinct."

"There's a girl at the station."

Kathryn shook her head. "You just made my point." They paused while the ME zipped the body bag.

"Hold on," Hayes interrupted. "We want to check something."

She pulled her phone, flipped to the image she managed to capture during the break in. The two men hovered on either side of her, looking from her image to the pale face of the dead man. "He's got red hair. Facial features are similar."

Hayes pointed at the body. "I don't see a scar on the man in the photo."

"Light's not the best. Close enough to be a match." She turned to the older ME. "What do you think? You're the expert."

He nodded. "I'd match him. What time did you take the picture?"

"Around midnight. He got himself shot between one and what? Five or six o'clock this morning?" She sighed. "He should have let Marshall nab him."

"Let's go tell the boss the good news." Hayes walked Kathryn toward the street.

The ME nodded at the attendants who finished zipping the bag. "I'll let you know if anything interesting shows up."

Marshall leaned against the front of the Escalade. Although the sun wasn't yet worth blocking, his sunglasses were in place. His arms were crossed. He looked the epitome of a dark hero waiting for combat. His lips barely moved in greeting, which didn't keep Kathryn from thinking how they fit against her own.

"Is it the perp from last night?"

At least his tone wasn't cold. She nodded. "I think I'll take you up on that coffee now."

He sighed. "Hop in."

"My jeeps down the street."

"Come up four blocks this way and turn right." He pointed north. "Coffee shop's on the corner."

"See you in a minute."

It took slightly longer, but he exited his vehicle as she pulled into the slot beside him.

~

The Coffee House door stood open when they arrived. An early morning server pulled a long cord from the table and chairs on the sidewalk. He moved to follow them, but Marshall held up his hand. "Just going to grab two cups. I'll pay you when you're done."

The young man waved, and Kathryn followed Marshall inside. The heavy scent of fresh-brewed coffee hung in the air. With a deep breath, she cleared some of the cobwebs from her mind. The kiss. She knew she shouldn't think about it, but her stomach curled in memory. Focus. Coffee. She should be irritated with the man, not wondering if the warmth of his mouth against hers was a fluke. She kept the coffee black. No need to sweeten the cup this morning. She chose a booth and scooted to the middle of the seat. He slid in across from her. “Think you’ll be able to identify the man?”

He pointed to his neck. “Had a tattoo like a snake. Could help.”

She grimaced. “Never a pleasant way to begin your shift.”

He raised his cup. “Irish cream. Takes the edge off.”

“Any sign this could connect to the shooting in the parking lot?”

“He was shot. Other than that—we need an ID to go on. MEs working on it.”

“What’s next on your agenda?”

“Richard.”

She took a drink. That made sense. She’d like to get a chance at him herself.

“No.”

He must have read something in her face. “Why not?”

“Because this isn’t your jurisdiction.”

“You’ve got a lot going on and a small crew to handle it. Why not let me help? I assure you, I’m competent.”

“I don’t doubt it.”

Yeah, right. She raised her brows. He had the grace to flush. “I don’t think you’re incompetent.”

“Then let me help. You need it.”

“Fine. When we find him, we may need to pull Jackie aside.”

“Protective of her son?”

"Just a tad."

Kathryn stood. "Let's go."

Marshall glanced at his watch. "It's still too early. The sun is barely up."

"Which makes this the perfect time. Especially if we catch him in REM sleep. Harder for him to focus on lies."

"I don't think— "

She placed her hand on his arm. "I need a lid," she nodded at the side table. Her grin broadened as he stood. Small victories. Instead of walking away from the table, he stepped closer to her. She retreated a step, but then there was nowhere else to go. He placed both their cups on the table.

"I think you're right, by the end of today you will drive me crazy." He kissed her, lingering on her lips until they tingled. Her hand crept to the curls at the base of his head. Oh, he kissed good. More than just her lips were tingling by the time he released her. He blinked, stunned. She could relate. She gave a little push. "Lids are over there." Kathryn wrapped her hand around her cup and headed for the jeep.

"Why don't we take mine?" Marshall stood beside the black SUV.

She breathed. Best to clear the air. "Something about you keeps me from being professional. This is my sister. I can't afford distractions."

"Agreed." He responded quickly. "Whatever is between us can go on a back burner. We're adults. We can work together."

She took a step toward him. He didn't have to agree so quickly. She gave herself a mental shake. He was right. They were both experienced cops. "Lord, this is a different sort of danger I don't want in my life." She muttered under her breath.

"What?" He opened the door for her.

"Nothing. Thinking out loud."

"Trait of a good cop." He shut the door.

~

The drive to Hutchins Apartments started out in silence. Kathryn twisted a piece of hair. What had she started? Her brain needed to focus on Lizzie, figuring out what happened to her, not on the hunk of man driving the SUV across town. She crossed her legs and stared out the window. Could Richard know what happened to Lizzie? Would Jackie protect her son? "How old is Richard? Jackie seems a bit dated to be going to his house to fix dinner."

"She must be close to seventy now. I think she had him late. He's only in his early thirties. He works construction. Part of it may be his way of keeping tabs on Mom. Beau died a few years ago. Jackie got lost for a while."

"Beau her husband?"

"Yes. Robert, technically. But everyone knew him as Beau. They were married thirty-two years."

"That's a long time, especially by today's standards."

"You don't see long-term marriage in your future?"

"I'm a cop. There are days I don't even see a future." She laughed. "You know how it goes. Normal people don't understand what we do. What we go through. Have you had a successful relationship?"

"I thought at one time."

"She didn't get it, did she?"

"I'm the one who didn't get it."

"Sure. Blame the cop." She shook her head. "What didn't you get?"

He pulled into the parking lot of the apartment building, and Kathryn wanted to slap herself. Why did she even care if his relationships worked out? He stopped in a parking space near the end unit, and she reached for the handle.

"I didn't understand that a relationship required time. Quality time. I believe that when the correct woman comes around, I'll be willing to put in the quality time necessary to make a relationship work."

She pushed the door open, then hesitated before exiting the vehicle. "I hope you find her." *But it isn't me. No way.* So why did her heart suggest otherwise?

Chapter 7

Marshall kept his hands shoved in his pockets. What was he thinking? Sharing his thoughts with her? A quick glance to the left, he saw her walking beside him, hair billowing with a passing breeze. Yes, attractive. Kissing her in the coffee shop had been a bad idea. But it felt right. How could he move the investigation forward if his brain wasn't willing to cooperate? He pounded his fist on the door. A bit harsh but his equilibrium had tilted, and he couldn't seem to regain the correct balance.

"Richard, what on earth do you think…" Jackie swung the door open. Her white hair poofed around her head. The house dress looked to be a few sizes too large and resembled a bright orange tent. The harried look on her face cleared into a smile. "Marshall." She looked at Kathryn. "And you brought your date again. Come in, so good to see you." She backed away from the door and motioned for them to enter. "Have you seen Richard? I swear that boy … doesn't matter if he's thirty or three, I'll whoop his backside for scaring me like this."

Marshall allowed Kathryn to enter in front of him and then he motioned Jackie into the living room. He shut the door. With the two women comfortable on the couch, he sat in an armchair. "Richard hasn't been home?"

"Not yesterday or last night. I can't imagine where he would go. If he had a new assignment out of town, he would have told me."

"After you called the police the other night, did you go back outside?"

"No. Richard said to stay inside. He wanted me to be safe. He's a good son. Usually."

"Could he have known the people in the parking lot?"

Her smile drooped, and she shrugged. Kathryn glared at him. She wrapped an arm around Jackie's shoulders. "If your son saw something that made him nervous, what might he do? Where would he go? A friend's house, perhaps?"

Jackie thought for a moment and then patted Kathryn's knee. "Of course, dear. Why didn't I think of that? The Hewitt boy." She looked at Marshall. "You know him, don't you?"

"Not since high school." He nodded.

"Very well." To Jackie, the matter was closed. Her face brightened, and she turned to Kathryn. "When this is over, dear, you'll have to give me an opportunity to shoot that gun of yours. I bet it has a real kick. And don't you worry, my Beau, he taught me to hold on."

"I would love to." Kathryn's eyes glittered with humor. She faced Marshall. "Hewitt's?"

He nodded. "Get some sleep, Jackie. If Richard comes home, give me a call."

The ride to the Hewitt's remained silent. Kathryn seemed lost in her thoughts, or the passing scenery held her spellbound. The trailer park maintained their grounds, landscaping the front entrance and encouraging homeowners to keep their yards pristine. The Hewitt place was on the main drag.

"Doesn't look like a bachelor pad." Kathryn leaned forward to see outside the windshield.

"Dan and Sarah Hewitt."

"Richard's not concerned about bringing trouble to his friends?"

"Dan hasn't always been on the straight and narrow. Besides, we don't know Richard's in trouble. He's a grown man. He's not required to head for home if he doesn't want to."

Marshall exited the car. When he reached the mauve-painted door, he managed to knock a bit more civilly. Sarah, a petite Kindergarten teacher, swung the door open at the first knock.

"Good morning, Marshall." She glanced at Kathryn and smiled.

Kathryn held out her hand. "Kathryn Brussels, I'm working with Marshall on an investigation."

Sarah's eyes widened. "An investigation? What brought you here?"

"We thought Richard might have spent the night."

She shook her head with a laugh. "Couch potato. Dan ran into him last night and thought he'd had too much to drink. Insisted on bringing him back here." She glanced at her watch. "Oh my, I have to run. Can't have sixteen five-year-olds wandering the playground unsupervised." She waved them in. "Through the kitchen."

Marshall and Kathryn entered. Apples and cinnamon floated through the air. The house had a warm family feel, though the couple had yet to welcome children into the fold. Bright yellow paint kept the kitchen sunny. A half-full coffee carafe and two empty mugs sat in the sink. Marshall moved around the center island toward the other door. The back room remained dark. He felt Kathryn standing beside him. The covers on the couch had been thrown into a haphazard pile. The pillow still had an indent from someone's head. But the couch was empty. Richard was gone.

"Now what?"

"We place a car outside his apartment. He'll have to go there at some point. I say we head back to the station." A clock on the wall chimed half past eight. "We should get reports coming in on our alley victim."

~

Three folders sat on the captain's monstrous desk. But not the one for which he waited. Kathryn picked up the one closest to her side. He held out his hand. "Would you like me to go snooping around your desk?"

"Just trying to help."

"How was staying at your sister's?"

"I kept the gun loaded. Cleaned up the mess your people left. Did they find anything useful dumping out the arts and crafts boxes?"

"Arts and craft boxes? I never heard anything about that. Anything in them?"

"Leather, silver studs, different sized jewels and beads."

"It had to have been the person in the house earlier."

She shook her head. "He never went into the third bedroom."

"I'll ask Officer Hayes about it; he directed the search."

"No need to get him in trouble. It's cleaned up now."

"Get who in trouble?"

Kathryn and Marshall turned toward the door. Officer Hayes stood, one hand poised to knock and the other carrying a slim folder.

Marshall straightened. "You have something?"

Hayes sent an uncomfortable glance at Kathryn. Her face lit, and Hayes' lips tightened.

Marshall waved in her general direction. "Luke, she's helping with the investigation."

"I didn't realize we needed help."

"I'm here to help my sister."

Hayes cleared his throat and tapped one hand against the red file from the morgue. "Pre-lim."

"What's interesting?"

"Prints came through." He read from a form. "Shawn McGowan. Wanted for questioning related to a jewelry heists in Philadelphia."

Marshall frowned. What was he doing in central Florida?

"A gang of at least five managed four robberies in as many months. No one injured."

"Do you have dates?"

"Eighteen months ago."

"And now his body shows up in a back alley in the middle of Florida?"

Kathryn leaned forward. “No connection to Lizzie?”

Hayes shook his head.

“Then why were you worried?”

Hayes shifted his eyes to Marshall, who shrugged. “Out with it.” He knew better than to try side-stepping Kathryn, even if he wanted to.

“We received a Jane Doe notice from a hospital in Tampa.”

She jumped to her feet. “They responded to the missing person’s report?”

“You know what Jane Doe usually means …” Hayes gulped.

Marshall felt the chill of her stare after she managed to silence Hayes. Marshall sighed. “Send the directions to the GPS in the chief’s SUV.” He stood, grabbed his jacket, and watched Kathryn plow around Hayes. With a shake of his head, he raced after her. “Hold up, Punk.”

“I don’t recall asking for your help.”

“This will go better if we work together. I need you to read the report and tell me what stands out. You have experience with gangs.”

Her eyes maintained their artic glare, but she accepted the folder.

A chill struck Marshall when he exited the building, even though sunlight brightened the sky and temperatures climbed close to seventy. Kathryn sensed it as well, her eyes darting from one side of the street to the other. He studied the cars parked along Main Street. The reflection of light in windshields prevented him from observing anything helpful. Hiding his eyes behind sunglasses, he peered at shop doorways and groups of benches arranged around large planters. Nothing stood out, but the uneasy feeling didn't disperse. He took Kathryn's elbow and steered her toward the black SUV parked in front of the station.

"Keep an eye on traffic. I want to know if someone follows us."

"You felt it too?" Her eyes were no longer cold, they were all business. He really had to stop noticing the nuances.

~

Kathryn flipped through images in her mind of the people she'd noticed. An older couple holding hands and ambling along the brick path. A mom with a stroller trying to hold a door and push into the store. A teenager who should be in school testing his skateboard in front of the closed ice cream shop. Mundane and ordinary, although why her heart tweaked at the site of the old couple, she didn't understand. No one followed the SUV. "Nothing and no one."

"Makes me more nervous." Marshall gave a quick glance out the rear-view mirror. "I want to see my enemy."

"We know this one." She tapped the folder. "Will you contact Philly PD?"

"I'll leave that to the ME."

She opened the folder and read through the printout. "Shot elsewhere and dumped in the alley. Not enough blood at the crime scene. He had a large square ring on his pinkie, white gold, couple carats. Wow."

"Must have been a piece he liked. Anything to connect him to your sister?"

Kathryn liked the way he drove with his eyes on the road while conversing but didn't care for his jump to conclusions. “Nothing. How can all this be related?”

“I don’t like coincidence.”

He said it like she should agree. She felt a wrinkle forming in her forehead. “Explain that one for me.”

“We have one person shot, the same man you saw break into your sister’s house. A community member thinks she saw someone else get shot. Her son is not being cooperative even though he must have witnessed something. We aren’t a big town, and the crime rate tends to be low. It makes sense the events are connected.”

“But you have no evidence. You’ll make judgments based on what you think and miss something.” Police work had to be objective. Couldn’t he see that?

“Teamwork makes the balance.”

She checked the side mirror, but nothing stood out. Her usual proclivity for argument faded.

“When was the last time you say your sister?”

Kathryn felt her shoulders tighten with Marshall’s quiet question.

He didn’t accept her silence. “It’s almost an hour’s drive, don’t want to spend the entire time with nothing to say.”

“Tell me something about you.” She still faced the window but could see his reflection.

He drummed his pointer finger on the steering wheel. “This is my first shot as acting captain. I keep thinking, what would Breyer do if he were here? Am I going to make solving this case harder? I don’t want to mess up and be a disappointment.”

Kathryn sighed. She understood disappointment. “Lizzie moved here because I worked in Lakeland.” She chuckled. “I couldn’t believe it. Shows up one day.

We haven't spent any real time together, not since college." Kathryn straightened in her seat. "We planned a day for the two of us to go exploring. But word came from Miami just before we left the apartment. I got assigned to an undercover team." She folded her arms over her chest. "It's what I've been working for. I know Lizzie was disappointed. Still, I did manage to eat breakfast with her." She'd hurried through breakfast, ignoring Lizzie's hurt because focus on work came easier.

"How long ago did that happen?"

"Months. I figured we can spend time together when this assignment is over. She'd still be there." Kathryn swallowed against the hard lump in her throat. Now what would she see? She couldn't imagine her sister's body devoid of life. She folded her hands together and squeezed until she felt pain. Marshall must have noticed. He stretched out his arm and placed his hand against her neck. The gentle motion of his fingers comforted.

"You can do this." The tone of his voice tried to break through the unpleasant thoughts rummaging in her head.

"Doesn't matter if I can or can't. It'll be what it is."

"I hope you see me as a friend and let me help."

What could she say? Who had time for friends? And did she want a friend like him? Their kisses felt more than friendly. She pushed the thought away. Her sister lying dead on a cold slab. That's what she needed to think about. Marshall's hand slipped away, and the chill of death loomed closer.

Chapter 8

The hospital teemed with life. Sick, broken life with noisy children. The elevator swooshed closed, and silence reined. Marshall pushed the appropriate button, but he kept his distance and didn't try touching her again. Shame, really. Kathryn stiffened her back. Treat it like a job. Focus on the here and now. She could do this.

The silence of the hallway to the morgue roared inside her head. She noticed the click of her shoes and the heavier tread of Marshall's. She didn't want to admit it, but his being there helped. She sought his hand for a quick squeeze and then pushed through the swinging metal doors.

She'd done this before, as the police officer, standing beside a family member in front of the wide window with drawn blinds. The horizontal rows lifted without a sound. The glass must be thick. She forced her mind to focus on the table, not the mundane where it seemed to want to stay. The air conditioner kicked in, but the touch of cold meant nothing. Her mind catalogued the features. Darker hair. Thinner lips. The shape beneath the white sheet too rounded. She shook her head. She thought she would be overwhelmed with relief, but all she felt was numb.

~

He had to agree the body wasn't Lizzie. Kathryn turned around and marched back to the hallway toward the elevators. He waved at the coroner and gave thumbs down before chasing after the ice princess. At least she held the elevator for him.

Her hand went up before he could speak. "Don't bother. It wasn't this one, but how many more girls are out there? How many more bodies will I get to see before it's Lizzie beneath the blanket?"

"I'm sorry."

She didn't say anything else. Exiting the elevator, his step faltered when the phone on his belt buzzed.

"Franklin."

"It's Brenda." He recognized the voice of the office dispatcher, but her voice shook with a sob.

"What's wrong?"

"Hayes was shot."

He stopped moving. "What? When? How?"

"They got an address on McGowan. That's all I know. The report of shots fired came in and then officer down." She sobbed again.

"Is he?"

"He's at Memorial. They won't tell me anything."

"I've got this. Let me find out. Hang in there."

He didn't bother with goodbye. Heart pounding, he searched the number of Memorial Hospital. His thumb shook as he pressed the call button. "This is Sergeant Franklin, PD. I got a report you have one of my officers." He held the phone to his ear, pressing his other hand against his eyes to blot out the distractions of the hospital. He felt a warm touch on his arm and knew Kathryn stood beside him. He couldn't look at her, could only wait for the dreaded news.

"They took him into surgery. The bullet nicked an artery. The prognosis doesn't look good, sir. He lost a lot of blood."

"I'm on my way. Anything he needs, he gets." He started walking.

~

Officer down. She'd experienced it herself, but not in such a tight-knit group.

"That poor girl. I wonder who she is."

The conversation captured her attention, and she turned slightly. Two nurses stood nearby. "Girl? You have another Jane Doe?"

The nurses clammed up, but Kathryn pulled out her badge. "Marshall," she yelled down the hallway. He seemed to realize she wasn't beside him and looked back at her. She could read impatience on his face, but she wasn't moving. He backtracked, clearly upset. She faced the nurses.

"You have a Jane Doe?"

"We don't call them Jane up here." The taller one glanced at her chart. "Hope. That's her name. She came in with a gunshot wound.

"Dumped in the ambulance bay is more like it." The other nurse scoffed.

"But her name is Hope?"

Marshall leaned closer. "We have to go, Kathryn. It's an hour drive back to town. Hayes could be dead by then."

"We don't know her real name. That's the one we gave her."

Kathryn heard both at the same time. She looked at Marshall. "They have another unidentified patient."

"I have to go, Kathryn."

"Fine. I'll get my own ride back to town."

"I can't leave you here. Don't you understand? I'm in charge. Hayes got shot on my watch."

"I do understand, but I have to check on this. I'll be fine."

"Five minutes." He growled, and she could feel anger rolling off him in waves.

The two nurses glanced uneasily from one to the other.

"Where is Hope?" she chose to ignore his bad attitude. She didn't want to feel the glimmer. What a ridiculous name. And why couldn't he accept the fact she was a seasoned officer? Capable of finding her own way back to the tiny blip of a town? Her feelings of angst bombarded with his.

They entered a small room where monitors beeped. A breathing machine hissed; its diaphragm lifted then pushed air through the tubes. The girl on the bed didn't look twenty-eight, she looked sixteen. Kathryn gulped, unprepared for the onslaught of emotion. Her knees went weak and she would have fallen if Marshall hadn't grabbed her. The anger between them faded to nothing. A choking sensation gripped her chest and a sob cracked through her lips. Horrified, she tried to beat any sign of emotion down. He set her in a chair and knelt in front of her, his warm hands rubbing hers. His eyes asked the question. She blinked and nodded. Blinked some more and felt tears roll down her cheeks. She'd been preparing herself to face Lizzie's death. Finding her alive, she wanted to cry, shout, and throw her arms around Marshall. Wiping her eyes, she rose and walked to her sister's bedside.

"What's her condition?"

The pair of nurses stepped to the other side of the bed. The taller one looked at the bed chart. "Medically induced coma. Shot in the abdomen. Infection. Serious, but she should recover."

"You said she was dumped? Did they see by whom?"

She shook her head. "There was an ambulance in the bay. The camera focused on it. She doesn't show up until it moves. You'll need to go to admitting and fill out her paperwork."

"No."

Kathryn turned on Marshall. "I said I can get a ride."

"It's not that. It's to protect *Hope*." He stressed her name.

"But she's my sister. I found her." Saying the words brought a smile to her face.

"And if you register her under her real name, the people who did this will find her and finish what they started."

She opened her mouth for another protest, but she knew he was right. Her sister remained pale and fragile, unaware of the debate surrounding her. She turned to the nurses. "You'll take care of her?"

They agreed. "Hope remains in our care. We have a wonderful ICU team. I'm Dottie." She pulled a business card from her pocket. "Here's the direct line." She tilted her head toward the desk where the phone sat. "Call for updates. We'll take good care of her."

Marshall's hand felt heavy on her shoulder. "Okay?"

With a final glance at her sister, she agreed. Marshall guided her to the hallway with his hand on her back. His pace calmed, and he led her through the throng of people. Lizzie lived. Every footstep seemed to chant, and she couldn't stop the smile of relief, even though she knew Marshall hurt for his officer. His soft grin told her he understood.

~

Marshall cut south of the main highway onto a county road to skip the slew of lights. With siren blaring, the vehicle topped seventy. Smaller cars and yard trucks moved over, and he made good time. Kathryn remained silent. Her relief was palpable, and if her reaction had surprised him, it seemed to shock her. Not such an ice princess after all. She interested him. The spark of attraction coursed between them, and he wanted to know more. But first, Hayes. The younger officer was relatively new, someone to take under his wing. They teased each other and carried on.

They arrived in town with his thoughts reeling. He drove directly to the hospital.

"Give me the keys," Kathryn ordered as he hit the brakes before running over the curb.

"Why?"

"I'll get details on what happened. Where he was, who was there. You're needed here, and you can't be in two places at the same time."

"But how?"

Her arched brows told him she didn't appreciate the question. How could he keep forgetting she worked undercover? He certainly hadn't forgotten their first meeting. He dropped the keys in her outstretched hand.

"Give me a call as soon as you learn something." He ordered, and she had the audacity to grin and wink.

"I'll be back before you know it."

He slipped out of the truck and held the door for her. For a moment, while she stood between the seat and the door, he thought about kissing her again. Her eyes sparkled, and he knew she recognized his thoughts. She kissed his cheek instead and pushed him away.

"Check on your officer." Reluctance slowed his steps, but he went anyway.

~

Kissing him now would be a huge mistake. Too many positive vibes buzzed through her body. She'd enjoy it and want to kiss him again. Oh wait, she already wanted to kiss him again. She closed the door and watched him walk into the hospital. Distraction from her job had never been an issue. This man in charge was trouble.

She went looking for answers.

Chapter 9

The radio beeped, and Kathryn connected without a thought. “Brussels.”

“Who?” The voice on the other end squeaked.

“Sergeant Franklin’s checking on Hayes. I’m running leads. What do you have?”

“Paisley’s Animal House and Animal Lodge both called to report break ins.”

“Send directions to the GPS and I’ll track them down.”

“Can you do that?”

“I’m a Miami Deputy. I think I can handle a couple break-ins at animal shelters.”

“Yes, ma’am, but are you allowed to?”

Kathryn sighed with frustration. “You have an officer down, a chief on vacation, and your sergeant is at the hospital. Are you hiding someone else?”

The female officer laughed. “Alright, smarty pants. I’m sending directions now. Have fun. You don’t have allergies, do you?”

Kathryn switched on the satellite program. "I hope not." She muttered when a steely voice from the GPS unit declared the first step. "Nice." Shaking her head, she backed the SUV from its place. She gave a final glance at the hospital. Smaller than Tampa's, yet people were fighting for their lives inside both. Her thoughts flew to her sister. "Don't you die on me, Lizzie."

She followed the navigator, but her thoughts remained with her sister.

~

Paisley's Animal House nestled between a coffee shop with the quaint name Joe's Cup, and a used bookstore, Betty's Best Books. The glass door of the animal shop had been shattered, yet the oversized window to the left remained intact. A pair of jade-colored eyes stared relentlessly from the narrow head of a Siamese cat. The regal creature sat on a pedestal and watched Kathryn walk along the sidewalk, determining her mettle. She resisted the urge to startle it.

Shards of glass littered the doorway, and she stepped through them carefully. Two women, both with white hair, stood with their backs to her whispering excitedly. One looked familiar.

"Jackie?"

Both whirled around, heads bobbing as they grabbed each other for support. Jackie's face brightened. "Kathryn. You shouldn't be here, dear. We're a bit of a war zone today."

"Paisley?" Kathryn addressed the other woman. When she nodded, she offered her badge. "I'm Office Brussels."

Jackie grabbed Paisley's arm, looking at the badge. "She showed me the most impressive weapon the other day." Jackie smiled, facing Kathryn. "Did you bring it today?"

Kathryn smiled. "I'm here to report on the robbery. Do you also work here?"

"Paisley and I have been friends forever. Can you imagine someone doing this?" She looked at Paisley. "In our town? And three days ago, I witnessed—" she shook her head. "Well, I'm not supposed to get into that."

Kathryn opened her small pad of paper to draw their attention. "What was taken?"

"That's the craziest thing," Paisley walked to the register and picked up a plain leather collar. "I'm missing these. The fancy ones with studs and jewels on them. They were different sizes for dogs and cats."

"I remember those." Jackie intervened. "Weren't they crafted by a local gal?"

"Her name?" Kathryn asked.

"She stamped her initials on the back of the leather." Paisley turned the plain collar over. "EB."

"She delivered them a few days ago. Those jewels she used could almost pass for the real thing. I would have bought the red, but I don't have a dog."

"They were lovely. I thought they'd do well during the Christmas season."

"What about the register?" Kathryn walked to the other side of the counter. The drawer on the classic register stood open. Beneath the counter, jumbles of boxes and partially opened packages filled the shelves. "Did they get in here?"

Jackie pointed her thumb at Paisley. "That's Paisley for you. She can tell you exactly what's where and how long it's been there." Jackie reassured with a pat on

Kathryn's shoulder. The other woman laughed.

"You should see my house if you think this is unorganized."

"The register?" Kathryn drew her attention once more.

"Oh yes. I mean no," shaking her head made her white curls bounce. "I took the drawer into the back office before locking up to go to lunch. There's no sign they were anywhere other than here."

"No money missing?"

Paisley sighed. "Strange things to take." Her eyes widened. "I hope EB doesn't expect me to pay her for the stolen articles."

"You said she's local? I can stop on my way to the Animal Lodge."

"Evelyn's place?" Both ladies looked surprised. "Oh, no."

Kathryn nodded.

Jackie's hands flew to her hips. "What are people thinking? They have a shoestring budget as it is. Running a shelter these days is a job for the heart, not the wallet." She bent and grabbed something from beneath the counter and stood. She clutched a red bag in her arms. "We'll get a group together right now and head over."

Kathryn noticed a van with the city emblem park at the curb. "Not yet. The crime unit just arrived. They'll dust for prints and then help you clean up the glass. You can't do anything for Evelyn until the unit finishes on her side."

Paisley took Jackie's bag and stuck it behind the counter again. She opened a drawer and held a card to Kathryn. "EB's. Her address is on the back."

Kathryn flipped the card and felt her stomach drop. The address on the back belonged to Lizzie. "Elizabeth Brussels? That's your artist?"

Paisley nodded. "Do you... oh, wait. Didn't you say your name was Brussels? Do you know her?"

"Yes, we're related."

Jackie brightened. "That will help."

"Not really. She's missing." Kathryn handed them both her own card. "Give me a call if you need anything. Don't mind the Miami address. Use the phone number." She smiled at the tech entering the store. "I'll head over to Animal Lodge."

"You tell Evelyn we'll be there as soon as we can. She's not alone." Jackie assured her.

Dog collars? Lizzie, what did you get yourself into? Kathryn opened the jeep door. Something reflected in the window, but when she turned to look, the area across the way was empty. Shivers cascaded down her back. The feel of being watched overwhelmed her. She slammed the car door. Years of undercover work taught her to watch for shadows, but this one eluded her. The jeep roared to life with the turn of her key, and Kathryn drove from town.

The GPS led her away from the gridded cross street area, and west. A few miles beyond town proper, she saw the sign for the Lodge. A faded dog on a large wooden plank swerved back and forth suspended from an arch with the words *Animal Lodge* printed in red below. A bumpy ride through the gravel-pitted driveway brought her around to the building. An old steel warehouse had been converted into an animal shelter. Pens with high fences surrounded the side and into the backyard. A lean-to had been attached to the front, allowing visitors reprieve from ill weather. The glass door leading into the front room had been shattered.

Unlike the pet shop, this place radiated with noise. A symphony of barks weaved through the air. Kathryn gripped her keys until the rough edge cut into her hand. Dogs were not her favorite. Pieces of glass crunched beneath her shoes. She crossed the threshold into the main room. The din of dog voices quieted. The woman behind the counter appeared frazzled, eyes rimmed with red and hands fluttering from one object to the next.

"Good morning." Kathryn offered a gentle smile. "I'm with the sheriff's department. Deputy Brussels." She held her ID. The middle-aged woman gave it a cursory glance without touching it. "Are you Evelyn?" Kathryn asked.

"Yes. I'm the one who called in this mess." She blinked. "Of all the stupid ... How can kids do this?"

"What makes you think kids were responsible?"

"They took collars." She pointed at her neck. "You know, the kinds with studs and fake jewels on them? Winters has glass in his paws. Why does he have to suffer because of their selfishness?"

"Winters?"

Evelyn leaned down and lifted a large beast that draped over her arm like a rug.

Kathryn bit her lip. "That's the largest cat I've ever seen."

"He's a Maine coon. Look at the poor thing." She held up one foot wrapped with gauze.

Dark hair peppered with silver blended with the cat's colors as Evelyn nuzzled the feline. "When I find one of those kids wearing my collar, I'll throttle him."

"That wouldn't be wise. Besides, kids might hit one place, but not two. Especially two this far apart."

"Two?" She looked up.

"Paisley's place downtown. Did you make those collars yourself?"

"No. I get them from an artist. She's new to town, but the work looks good."

"Which artist?"

Evelyn pressed her fingers against her temple and her eyes looked down and to the left. She tapped twice. "Oh, yes. EB. She has her initials stamped on the back of all of them."

"Elizabeth Brussels?"

"Yes." Lizzie brightened. "How did you know?"

"The same thing happened at the other store. Anything else missing? Money? Tampering with the register?"

"Brutus has the cage in front of the office. They'd have to be fools to try to get through there."

"So, the office is fine?"

She nodded. "I came through the back around ten. I take care of the dogs. It wasn't until I went looking for Winters, I found what happened."

Kathryn glanced around the store. Three large bins contained a variety of toys. Shelves held food and biscuits. A couple of cages precariously perched atop the shelves. "Do you have any collars left?"

"No." Evelyn frowned. "I had them all displayed by the register."

"Has anyone bought one?"

"I just put them out. EB brought them on Friday." The cat dropped from her arms and slithered behind the counter. "Oh, but I think Callie took one."

"Callie?"

"Our groomer. She was here when EB dropped by. Callie fell in love with a red one. She complimented it so highly, EB let her have it."

"Is Callie here?"

"Not for a few more hours." Evelyn stepped behind the counter and lifted a small basket. She began to rummage. "I know it's here somewhere. Ah, here we go." She handed a card to Kathryn. "Cell phone and address are on the back."

"Did anyone else know Callie took a collar?"

"I don't see how they would."

Kathryn looked at the card. The address should be on her way back to town. "I'll stop by, see if I can get a look at the collar."

"Should I give her a call, let her know you're on the way?"

"I wanted to take a walk around first. I'll call her when I get going." She checked her watch. "It'll be a while before the crime unit gets here. They were just getting started at Paisley's place when I left."

"I've got stalls to muck and animals to feed. Two assistants are waiting at the back gate. Can I let them in?"

"As long as they don't come up here. Should be fine."

Evelyn held out her hand. "Good to meet you, detective."

"Kathryn."

"Thank you, Kathryn."

Kathryn pulled her sunglasses from her jacket pocket while she stepped through the doorway. Dirt covered the ground closest to the pens and no sign of recent foot traffic could be seen. She continued around to the back. Several runs had been built. Everything looked in order. The thieves had stuck with the front room. Security? With a slap to her forehead, she hurried back.

Evelyn stood in the doorway leading into the back warehouse holding Winters.

"I forgot to ask about security. You don't have an alarm?"

"No. I figure the dogs cause enough racket."

"How far is your nearest neighbor?"

"Well, there's Mr. Reece down the lane. He's about half a mile. Follow the road almost a mile further south and you'll find Elmer's place. But he's deaf as a doorknob. Wouldn't do you any good asking him questions."

Kathryn smiled. "You're very helpful, Evelyn. I'll check with Marshall, see if he wants to talk to the neighbors."

Chapter 10

Marshall hovered in the admitting area of the hospital, his thoughts raging between Kathryn's stubborn determination and Hayes' condition. How was he supposed to focus when thoughts of her trapped between him and his door kept interrupting? At least the animal ladies would keep her out of trouble. He hoped. "And my SUV better not have a scratch."

The lady behind the computer glanced at him. He smiled and moved away. Talking to himself out loud. Just what he needed. A figure moved into and out of his peripheral vision and he turned. Brenda slunk around the corner, outside the rotating front doors. He jogged after her.

"Brenda."

She turned, her face twisted with guilt and concern. "They wouldn't tell me anything on the phone. I wanted to run in to ask and head back to the office."

"It's alright. He'd want you here." He motioned toward the door.

Her eyes filled with tears. "How could he let this happen?"

"I don't think he did it on purpose."

"I know." She hiccupped. "But he should be more careful."

"He will. Getting shot once is enough to do that." The whir of the door separated them. She stood at the check in, handing over her ID by the time he caught up to her.

"Where do we go?" She placed the sticker on her jacket lapel. Straight and tidy, like Brenda always was.

"There's a sitting room on the second floor. They have coffee and tea available. I prefer the lobby."

She looked at the wide set of windows. "Keep an eye on your world."

"I'm still in charge of it, even though we're in here."

She took a step toward the door, her face once again swathed with guilt. "I should go back to the office."

"You're fine." He took her by the shoulders and turned her to face the elevators. "Go upstairs." She obeyed. Which was more than Kathryn would do. He groaned and returned to pacing the glistening-clean tiled lobby floor.

~

"He's a lucky man. The bullet nicked his shoulder and turned outward. A different trajectory might have sent it through his chest."

"We get the picture, Doctor." Marshall glanced at Brenda.

The doctor cleared his throat. "He's out of surgery. We've repaired the damage to his shoulder. He'll be here a few days, then rehab."

Brenda clenched her hands together. "Can we see

him?"

"Are you family?"

"She's part of the police force."

The doctor shrugged. "Guess that makes you family." He winked. "Short visits. One at a time." He wagged a finger at Brenda. "No getting all weepy on him. He's out of it now, but he'll wake up in a few hours."

Marshall took the first visit. Machines beeped, and the florescent overhead light made Hayes appear gaunt. Sallow skin pulled tight across his face. His shoulder and upper torso had been wrapped in gauze, immobilizing him. Marshall's lips twitched upward as he pulled his cell phone from his pocket. He shouldn't. He snapped a picture anyway. It would come in useful some time.

"Heal quick, buddy. It's not like you to leave the department shorthanded." Thank you, God. The boy breathed on his own. Alive. Relief surged through him. He couldn't wait to tell Kathryn. Where had that thought come from? He rubbed the back of his neck, turning to leave. "Go ahead, Brenda."

The young woman rushed past, and he didn't hear any gasping or unexpected cries. He smiled. Hayes was in for a surprise. He stopped at the nurse's station. "Let her know I went to the lobby to make a phone call." The older woman nodded.

He took the stairs rather than wait for the elevator.

"How is he?" Kathryn answered on the second ring.

"He'll live. Until I get my hands on him for getting shot."

"I'm glad it's good news."

"What have you found out?"

Kathryn updated him on her observations at both locations. “I'm on my way to Callie's. She's the groomer for Animal Lodge. Lizzie gave her a collar on Friday. She may have the only one not in the hands of thieves.”

“Lizzie? Your sister, Lizzie?”

“Yes. My twin is apparently into arts and crafts. Although I never knew. She designed the collars at both locations. The only things taken at both locations.”

“That doesn't make sense.”

“Tell me about it. This is one quirky little town you've got here.”

“Did they say anything else?”

“Evelyn says she has a neighbor about half a mile who may have heard something. I was going to call you.”

“Animal Lodge?” He thought a moment, a map of the area moving in his head. “Reece’s place. Alistair Reece. He's an old timer, but a good man. I'll drop in on him. He's probably missing the Captain by now. I think Breyer visited half a dozen old-timers on a regular circuit.”

“Sounds like a good man.”

“You'll have to stick around and meet him when he gets back.”

Kathryn said nothing, and Marshall covered his eyes. What was he thinking? Oh wait, he wasn't.

He heard the door shut, and then she responded. “I'm not going anywhere until I know what happened to Lizzie.”

“Give me a call when you finish with Callie. I'll meet you in town.”

“Want me to drive by the hospital to pick you up?”

He considered the possibility, but things had heated

quickly the last time with her in the same vehicle. "Nah, Brenda's here. She wanted to see Hayes for herself. I'll ride with her to the station."

"I didn't realize they were an item."

"I don't think Hayes realizes it yet either."

She laughed. "Goodbye." The phone clicked, and their tenuous connection abruptly ended.

~

Kathryn followed directions from the shelter back into town. A different part of town. Callie lived close to the trailer park, but the cracked road bounced the SUV. Weeds spilled over into the street and fences looked rundown. The masculine GPS voice indicated the house. A clothesline hung between the posts for the carport. Country music drifted through an open window. After parking on the ruts in the lawn, Kathryn tried the front door, but her knocking couldn't be heard over the din of music. She walked around the side. An older woman leaned over the edge of the rail of the back deck, banging a carpet against the wood.

Kathryn waved. "Good afternoon."

The woman offered a hesitant smile. A dog began barking through the back door. "May I help you?"

Kathryn showed her the badge. "I'm working with the police. Did you hear about the animal shelter this morning?"

She nodded. "Awful. How can anyone do such a thing? There, of all places. What will happen next?"

"Hopefully our investigation will catch the culprits. Evelyn said you received a collar from Lizzie Brussels?"

Her forehead wrinkled. "Who?"

"The artist that brought collars to the shelter last

week, EB. She offered you one for your dog."

"Oh, the dog collar. It's beautiful."

"May I see it?"

Callie opened the back door, and a little mutt wiggled its way through the space. Kathryn's feet were attacked by a pink tongue. Laughing, she lifted the animal. Callie unhooked the collar. They traded. Kathryn studied the collar. The leather strap, about six inches long, had three triangular studs and three red rubies in silver settings. Glittering rubies. Real? "May I keep this? Just for the investigation."

"Keep?"

"Borrow. Bands like this were stolen at a store in town and at the shelter. I will personally be sure it is returned to you." Kathryn pet the small dog and it attacked her hand with tiny teeth and a scratchy tongue.

Carrie gave the pup a playful shake. "Alright. If it will help."

"I will make certain it gets returned to you." Kathryn wrapped the collar in a napkin and placed it in a compartment inside her purse. "There. Safe and sound."

Kathryn pulled her cell from her shoulder bag after she stepped into the SUV. She meant to call the switchboard but noticed Marshall's name in her contact list. She pressed call. When had he added his number to her phone? Why did the act make her feel something akin to butterflies? She fought the unexpected attraction while listening to his phone ring.

"I've been waiting for you."

His sultry voice made her grip the steering wheel tighter. "What?"

"Brenda's heading to the office. I'll cross over to Palace. We can meet there."

"Where?"

"Palace Pizza. You like pizza, right?"

"Who doesn't?"

He laughed. "Those who are untrustworthy. What's your ETA?"

She turned right heading downtown. "I'm close, I think. I swear, these small towns are harder to navigate than Miami. I'll pull over in a minute and get the address."

"Are you on Broadway?"

She read the sign at the intersection. "I think so."

"Keep heading south, away from the highway. The pizza place is on the left once you pass the courthouse."

It didn't take long to find. Kathryn turned the corner and found a place to park. The butterflies didn't improve, and the itch between her shoulders warned the presence of the mysterious shadow. She walked inside the restaurant. The smell of fresh pizza triggered her hunger, but she paused at the door, watching. The few figures moving on the sidewalks did not seem out of place.

"Everything okay?" Marshall stepped close enough she could feel him even though they didn't touch. "Something's not right. I feel as though I'm being watched."

She looked at him. "Starting a few days ago?"

He shrugged. "Can't tell if it's this case or another completely different." He took a step back. "Let's eat."

After they ordered a couple of slices at the counter, Marshall pointed to a table where his open laptop sat. "I already have my drink."

Kathryn used the moment by herself to get sweet tea and take a few deep breaths. Marshall affected her. No reason to deny it. But for the sake of Lizzie and Hayes, she needed to focus on the case, not on the hunky sergeant. She silently groaned. Thinking of him as hunky would *not* help.

~

When Kathryn Brussels joined him at the table, Marshall noticed a touch of heightened color in her cheeks and an unwillingness to focus on him. Her eyes darted around the restaurant where a few other patrons enjoyed a late lunch or early supper. She also watched outside through the large glass windows. "Everybody okay at the animal shelter and pet store?"

"They were understandably shaken. Jackie was at the pet store. She's close with the owner."

"Did she say anything about Richard?"

Kathryn shook her head, causing the soft waves of her hair to move. He forced his attention to her face.

Kathryn pushed her straw through the plastic lid causing a squeak. She didn't seem to notice his distraction. "Has Hayes talked about what happened? Who shot him?"

"No." Marshall leaned back. An Italian waiter brought their slices. He waited until the man walked away from their table. "Surgery knocked him out. Brenda didn't even want to stay long. I'll get his statement in the morning."

"He's out of the woods?"

"He'll recover. No major damage done. You said you were stopping at Callie's?"

Kathryn covered her mouth with her hand, chewing her first bite of pizza. "That's really good."

"Authentic," Marshall agreed.

Kathryn reached for her purse, pulled something from an inside pocket, and handed it to him. "It's the collar Callie got from Lizzie."

"You think it's important?"

"Take a look. I'm not a jewel expert, but those look like quality."

He opened the tissue. "Metal studs?" Then he noticed the twinkle of a red jewel. "Oh, wow. I see what you mean." He glanced at her. "Do you think your sister knew these were real?"

"We don't know they're real."

"There's a jeweler next block up. He'll know." He covered the collar and put it in the breast pocket of his white shirt. They ate in silence for a moment, but he couldn't keep from taking the opportunity to get to know her. "Was Miami your first time working undercover?"

"I've had special assignments ever since academy. Lakeland, and then Miami, it all fell into place."

"You didn't grow up in Miami?"

"We're from Tennessee. Moved around a lot. Ended up in school in Virginia."

"I'm a true Florida cracker. Got as far as Tallahassee for school, but my parents were in this area."

"Are they still here now?"

"Their address is here. They're on a six-month tour of Europe."

"What?"

"I know. I think they're currently in Germany."

"I can't imagine what that must be like."

"Perk of retiring early. What about your folks? Did

you let them know about Lizzie?"

Kathryn looked down at her plate and picked at a slice of pepperoni. "Our parents are dead. It's just us."

"I'm sorry. I didn't know."

"Of course not. I don't walk around with an orphan sign on my chest. How late do you think that jeweler will be at his shop?"

Marshall glanced at his watch. "It's almost four. We should have plenty of time to head over there. You may want to try some cannoli first."

"We can save desert for later." She finished her last bite of pizza. "What's on the computer?"

"Waiting on reports. TV shows make the process seem faster."

"Don't get me started. If you're done, let's see what the jewelry store has to offer."

He held up the heel of his second slice. "Not quite."

Kathryn grabbed the heel from Marshall, pulled it into two pieces, handed half back and ate the other half herself. "Really good. My treat next time."

Marshall closed his computer and grinned. Sassy woman.

~

Kathryn knew they arrived when she saw the iron bars on the front windows. The owner talked with another customer, a tall man with dark features. The man peered at Kathryn, lips thinning, before returning his attention to the older jeweler. Kathryn followed Marshall to a display case. She watched the other people in the shop through the reflective glass.

"What do you think of diamond tennis bracelets?" Marshall pointed.

"I'm more likely to break the hook and lose…" she

peeked at the price tag then lowered her voice to a whisper. "Nearly a thousand dollars? Are you kidding me?"

The other man glanced in their direction before he left. It wasn't a curious or cursory look. He seemed to recognize her, but she'd never met him. Which meant he knew Lizzie.

"How may I help you folks? Got a special occasion in mind?"

Kathryn's eyes widened. "Oh no."

Marshall swallowed a chuckle, pulling out his badge. "We need your expert opinion on something. I'm Sergeant Franklin. This is Detective Brussels." He pulled the collar from his pocket, crumpling the tissue in his other hand. "We'd like you to look at this."

"Oliver Hughes." He provided his name, then pulled the collar from Marshall's hand. "A dog collar? What would I want with this?"

"It's evidence, actually. We'd like you to look at the red jewels. Are they real? Synthetic or fakes?"

"Red ones?" The collar dangled from his hand. His brows raised when his gaze settled on the gem. "Ah." He pulled a jeweler's glass from his pocket, squeezing his right eye around it. He pulled the collar close, carefully studying the jewel. "The quality is remarkable. Possibly a carat and a half, which is a good size for an oval-cut gem." He looked at them. "This could easily be worth ten thousand."

Marshall nodded at the collar. "There's three of them on it."

"Three?" Oliver choked, then ran his finger across the leather, touching the sides of each ruby. "They're remarkable. What are they doing on a dog's collar?"

"Where would someone get gems of this quality?"

"Without a setting? The biggest houses are in New York, Philadelphia, and Los Angeles. If we're talking Europe, there's London and Paris."

Marshall opened his hand, shaking the tissue. Oliver gave him a look. "You don't wrap thirty thousand dollars' worth of rubies in a tissue." He walked to the counter and pulled a leather bag from underneath. "Here."

Kathryn watched the exchange, trying to breathe. Where had Lizzie gotten the rubies? What was she thinking? Had the other collars contained precious gems? Marshall tucked the leather pouch in his pant pocket. She followed him from the store.

"What was your sister doing before moving to town?"

"Customer relations, I think. She worked for Avis or Enterprise, one of those rental places."

"Any reason or way she could have this kind of merchandise?"

Kathryn shoved her hands in her pockets. Hearing Marshall voice the same questions running through her mind grated on her nerves. "I have never had any reason to think Lizzie wasn't an upstanding citizen. She's always been honest."

"Until now."

"You forget, she called me. Something had her spooked."

"In over her head."

"Obviously."

"I'm going to lock this up. Not much we can do until tomorrow. Hayes' statement, first thing."

"Anybody seen Richard yet?"

He shook his head. “Not that I’ve been notified. Let me give you a ride to the house. Make sure everything’s okay.”

“Not necessary.”

“I know, but I’m a southern gentleman, and it’s something I need to do for my peace of mind.”

It wasn’t his peace of mind that concerned her.

~

Marshall paused at the door of the hospital room to observe the officer on the bed. The whiteness of yesterday had turned to pale. Hayes reached to scratch something on his shoulder, and then winced. Marshall stepped into the room. “Better not pull any of those stitches,” he warned.

The man jumped, winced again, and then offered a hint of a smile. “Are you a doctor now too?”

Marshall wrinkled his nose. “And deal with blood and guts all day? No, thank you. I like my humans best when they’re in one piece with no holes.”

“You mean you don’t like me presently?”

Marshall moved closer. “I appreciate your service and sacrifice. And I’m thankful you’re alive, looking better in fact. Ready to talk about what happened?”

Hayes pressed a button on the bed remote to raise himself to a sitting position. The effort cost him, but he seemed more content once he adjusted his position. “You had me watching the apartment. That Richard guy slunk through the parking lot with about as much grace as an excited puppy. I followed him up the stairs.” He held up his hand before Marshall could say anything. “I know. I should have called it in and waited for back up. I swear the man looked more scared than anything. Firing the gun seemed to shock him.”

"So, it was Richard?"

Hayes nodded. "I didn't even have my weapon drawn. As soon as he saw what he'd done, he called for help."

"He'll be even harder to find now. I got to bring him in and get this sorted."

"Does the chief know?"

Marshall frowned. "He's unreachable. Next time he decides to do this, I'm hiding a satellite phone in his bag. There's still a week until he returns."

Hayes looked beyond Marshall. A moment later, Brenda entered the room with a bouquet of flowers. She grinned at Marshall and then widened her smile for Hayes. "Before you say anything, I would have gotten you a survival pack with beef jerky and root beer. This is from the others at the station." She wiggled an envelope. "You even got a card from your old job in Philly."

"A card?" Hayes took the vase with flowers first, giving it an appreciative smell. "Much better than hospital scent." He took the card with his other hand, giving a cursory glance and laying it on the bed beside him. "Things quiet down at the office?"

Brenda nodded. "I can do without this sort of excitement the rest of my life." She stepped back, but Hayes grabbed her hand.

"I appreciate what you did. You kept a level head and sent help fast."

She blushed, and then wrapped her other hand around his for a moment. Her color heightened more. She peeked at Marshall, dropping Hayes' hand. "I better head back." She walked across the room, slowing when she passed Marshall. "Don't you wear him out."

Marshall grinned at Hayes, who rolled his eyes. "I think we're done. I'll put a bolo out on Richard. With a little help from our neighbors, we'll get him. You," he tipped his head at Hayes, "get some rest. Follow doctor's orders and don't pester your nurses."

"Wow. Not sure how much of that I'll actually remember to do."

"Rest and get better. That's an order. I need you back on your feet."

"Yes, boss."

"I told you not to call me that." Marshall left, both grinning. Sense of humor must be a good sign. Finding Richard would be trickier. He needed to speak with Jackie.

With the apartment off limits while CSU gathered evidence, Marshall headed to Jackie's house on the west side of town. He drove the street first, and then drove several streets on either side. Nothing seemed amiss. Richard could be hiding at his mother's or planning to head there. Marshall found a place to park one street over. Walking to the front door of Jackie's house, he heard music, something from the forties sounding like Sinatra. He rang the bell when his knock received no response. A few seconds later, Jackie opened the door. She was still a pretty woman, even though in her seventies. Her hair had a reddish tint and looked recently groomed.

"Officer Franklin," she greeted. "Lovely to see you. Hayward should be home soon."

Marshall's stomach dropped. If Jackie waited for Hayward, her mind wasn't where it should be. Hayward had been dead ten years at least. "Is he out with your son?"

"Richie?" She shook her head. "That boy. Got himself in trouble at school. Again."

"He's out of school now, though. Right?"

"Out?" Jackie puzzled for a moment, and then her face cleared. "Of course. How silly of me. I do wish he would go to college. So much he needs to learn about the world."

"He's going to find the world is a bit rougher for him. Perhaps if I find him first, I can help."

"Find him? I didn't know we lost him." She glanced at her watch and frowned. "I can't image what is keeping Hayward. They should be back by now."

"I like the music you're playing. Are you planning to go dancing with Hayward?"

Jackie turned and walked from the foyer of the house to the kitchen. Marshall followed. As they entered the kitchen, Jackie did a slow spin, causing the skirt of her calf-length dress to bell for a moment. She had a dreamy smile on her face when she turned toward him. "We love to dance, you know. He took me for ballroom lessons. They said we were lovely together."

"I bet you were. He cared about you a lot, didn't he?"

She sank onto a bar stool at the counter. The pure happiness faded away. "He loved me. Hayward has always loved me."

"To the end and beyond?" Marshall asked softly.

Jackie's smile turned wistful. "And beyond. Some days it feels like he's right here with me."

"Especially those days you need his support? A day like today, perhaps?" He leaned across the counter and took her hands with his. "The past couple of days, some bad things have happened."

She blinked, squeezing his hands. "Something happened with Richard. I don't understand. He was pale and shaking. I told him to get help, but he swears there is no help for him."

"Do you know where he is?"

"Right here." Richard said from behind.

Marshall spun, reaching for his holstered weapon, but Richard held up his hands.

Jackie moved from the counter, went around Marshall, and wrapped her arms around her son. "You've found courage. I always knew you had it in you." When she turned back to Marshall, her eyes glimmered, but the dreamy look had faded. "You watch over him."

"I'm going to do my best." Marshall hardened his face and his attention turned to Richard. The man sighed, shoving his hands into his pockets. Marshall motioned for Richard to head for the door. "Let's take a ride in my car. I've got some questions to ask you."

They walked to the front of the house. Jackie held the door for them. She placed her hand on Marshall's arm. "Wait, this is the best part." She tilted her head to listen better. *I did it my way* swam through the air around them. Her hand dropped away.

"Lock up behind us. I'll call you later." Marshall promised, and then he and Richard left the house. "I'm parked next block over. Don't do anything foolish."

Richard remained grimly silent but kept pace beside Marshall.

Chapter 11

"Do you understand these rights as I've explained them to you?"

"Yeah, I understand." Richard hunched in the chair and looked at the closed door.

"Then you better start talking."

"Or I wait for my public defender." He lifted his wrist. "City Hall should have someone assigned by Monday afternoon."

"You shot a police officer, Richard. You don't want me to send you to county lock up. Talk here where I can protect you."

Richard's voice rose with frustration. "I'm not the one needing protection."

"Who then?"

Richard stood, knocking the metal chair to the floor. "Who do you think?"

"Sit down." Marshall remained calm. He sensed fear beneath the agitated outburst. "You aren't making sense."

The other man sat with a grunt, arms folded across his chest.

Marshall flicked a pen between his fingers, waiting until Richard glanced at him. "You can't mean your mother had anything to do with shooting officer Hayes."

Emotions flickered across his face until Marshall recognized capitulation. Richard leaned forward. "They threatened her. You want me to explain what's going on, you get Mom safe." He waited for Marshall to respond, his gaze steady.

Marshall nodded. "I'll speak with Jackie."

"No, you get her out of town. Somewhere safe. They said they'd kill her."

"Who?"

Richard went silent. He leaned back in the chair and crossed his arms again. By the thin line of his lips, Marshall could tell he'd get nothing further. "You won't have much time. Be ready when I get back."

Marshall ran his hand through his hair before he exited the room. What had Richard scared? He glanced at the hallway and felt a tug in his chest. Kathryn leaned against a counter chatting with Brenda. With one leg bent and a foot dangling in the air, she slapped her sandal against her foot by rocking her toes back and forth. Since when did he notice toes? He waited for the unusual sensation to pass, but his attention simply drifted upward. Both ladies turned in his direction and he pasted a benign smile on his face. What about her drew him? Not even Allison, his ex-fiancé, had managed to divert his attention so quickly.

"I have two reports on the break-ins."

He rubbed his neck with one hand and motioned toward the front door with the other. "I have to speak to Jackie. Join me and we'll swap news."

She fell into step beside him. "How is Jackie?"

"Not going to be pleased I've arrested her son," he sighed as they exited the building. Early afternoon traffic bustled along Main Street.

"You sure about him?"

"Hayes confirmed it. He has no reason to lie."

"Poor Jackie."

"Richard claims someone threatened her. He wants her in protective custody before he talks."

"Jackie won't like that."

"Another reason I brought you along."

"Here I hoped it was for my looks."

He coughed. "That too. What's up with the robberies?"

"Both locations were clean. No useable prints, not even shoes. Rules out the idea that kids were responsible."

"I think we knew professionals were involved once Oliver confirmed the red jewels were genuine rubies."

"All of them must have looked real." Kathryn tapped her fingers against her cell phone. "What if that's what this is about. Lizzie got her hands on real jewels."

"The money in her apartment suggests she knew they were real."

"There you go, making leaps again."

"How is that a leap? She has real gems. She has money. She got herself shot. Somehow, she crossed paths with a gang of jewel thieves. I told you these cases were connected."

"But we don't know how. You're asking me to think my sister did something illegal."

He pulled the SUV into a driveway and shifted to

park. He twisted in his chair to face Kathryn. "Right now, I have to go explain to Jackie that her son shot a police officer. That is not conjecture. That is a fact. And then, I have to convince her to leave town and let her son go through this on his own. If you want to help, join me. If not, hopefully Richard will enlighten both of us."

Kathryn exited the vehicle and slammed the door.

~

Lizzie had gotten herself into trouble, Kathryn could see that. But she knew her sister. No way did she cheat or steal. It wasn't her. Anger caused her blood to steam as she followed Marshall along the path to Jackie's apartment.

"My dears, how pleasant to see you again so soon." Jackie called from a flowerbed. Kathryn ran to her side to help her rise. "Thank you, the knees aren't as spry as they used to be." She looked from one to the other. "I thought you weren't an item, yet here you are, together again."

"We're working, Jackie." Marshall sounded frustrated.

How many other officers did he kiss? Or would it be rude to ask? Kathryn swallowed her giggle. How did this man manage to throw her emotions so easily? She felt a hand on her arm.

"Are you alright?" Jackie asked.

"Fine. We need to talk with you."

"Let me get cleaned up. Marshall knows where the glasses are, there's fresh tea on the counter. I'll take one as well." Jackie hobbled past them both, pulling her gardening gloves from her hands.

"Guess you're fixing me tea. Lots of ice, I like mine cold." With a triumphant grin, she followed Jackie through the front door and found the sitting room.

A few minutes later, Jackie joined her, followed by Marshall with a tray holding three glasses of tea. Jackie took the right side of the couch and rested her arm in a slight indent. She accepted the tea with a polite smile.

"Before you say anything, I must warn you, I already know about Richie. Mrs. Gertie insisted on being the first to tell me. You know that woman had the gall to sit at my kitchen table eating one of my muffins and tell me she knew he would amount to trouble? I had to take my frustrations out on somebody, and the flowerbeds took their toll."

"I know you love your son, Jackie." Marshall remained standing. Kathryn tried to catch his eye, but he ignored her.

"Of course, I do."

"He's involved. I won't know how much until he talks."

Kathryn cleared her throat. "Why don't you sit down, Sergeant Franklin, and save our necks?"

"We don't have much time."

"Sit." She used a firm tone and was pleased to see him arrange his body on the edge of Jackie's flower-covered divan. Kathryn turned her attention to Jackie. "Richard thinks you're in danger. He wants to help with the investigation but won't until he knows you are no longer in harm's way."

"You didn't arrest him?"

"I had to, Jackie." Marshall shot a dark glance toward Kathryn.

"You don't look like the kind of woman who wants the truth sugar-coated. Richard's in trouble, and he'll have to do time. But he wants to help. He's just worried you'll get caught in the crossfire."

"Thank you dear, but I don't have anywhere else to go. He's all I have."

"You have an entire town, Jackie. Problem is we need to get you out of town."

"I have the perfect solution." Kathryn leaned forward. "There's a friend in Tampa who needs someone to look over her. I'll arrange a hotel for you."

"Bad idea," Marshall growled.

"It's workable." Kathryn assured him.

Jackie placed her glass on a coaster. "I'll pack a small bag. Now Marshall, you know I love helping, but I'll only go if you both agree." She walked past, taking a moment to pat his cheek. "I know my Richie has his faults, but he isn't evil."

Jackie left the room and Marshall flopped back against the cushions. He rubbed both hands over his face.

She didn't want to wait for him to decide to speak. "What are your objections?"

"Are you daft? Richard may well be responsible for putting your sister in the hospital."

Kathryn jerked to her feet. "Having two things we want to keep secret in one place makes sense to me."

"I don't like your idea of sense." Marshall followed her. "Who will be there to protect them if trouble shows up?"

"Get Richard to talk and I'll go. We have to know what's going on."

"Jackie matters to people. I don't want her to get hurt."

She waved her arms. "Lizzie doesn't matter? Hayes? You don't think those two bodies lying in the morgue mattered to anyone? It's a broken world we're living in, and innocent people get hurt. Wicked people get hurt, too. We do our best to protect and leave the rest to God."

"I know." He rubbed his face again. "It's never been easy."

"Try anyway." Kathryn breathed, willing her agitation to calm. "We get Jackie to Tampa and Richard explains."

"I don't want them there on their own."

She pulled a hand through her hair. "I'll call in a favor. JD can watch the pair of them."

"Who's JD?"

"James Devereaux, a friend from Miami."

"We don't need to involve an ex-boyfriend."

"Boyfriend? Ha. I don't need that kind of trouble in my life. Don't get me wrong, he's a good man."

"I want to meet him before I leave someone from my town in his care." Her hard look increased his blood pressure. "What?"

"You're all cute when you go protective." Kathryn grinned wider as red touched the tip of his ears.

Marshall narrowed his eyes. "Help Jackie. Tell her to put the bag in the trunk while the garage is closed. Let's not announce to whoever's watching we're moving her to a different location."

Kathryn returned with Jackie within five minutes. He cleared his throat. "Come to the café around two like you would on a regular day. We'll get you out of town safely."

"And Richie?" Jackie looked hopeful.

"I'll do my best for him. You know I will."

"That boy." She shook her head. "No more excuses.

He made a mistake. I'll have to trust God that he'll redeem Richie somehow."

"Be careful." Kathryn gave her a hug. She grabbed her phone from her back pocket as they exited the house.

Marshall paced the sidewalk while Kathryn pressed numbers into her phone. Her eyes followed him back and forth.

"Earth to Brussels." James Devereaux spoke.

The familiar voice barking in her ear pulled her from the trance. "Sorry. Got sidetracked for a moment." Was Marshall smiling? "Did you complete the Gilroy report?"

"Signed, dated, and sealed. What do you need?"

Kathryn checked the street but saw no one. "My sister's been shot, and someone's threatened an elderly witness. They need a guardian."

"Where?"

"Tampa."

"Why haven't I heard about the new case?"

"It's off the grid. I didn't know Lizzie got herself into trouble, and I won't leave her here alone."

"How long are we talking?"

"A few days."

He laughed. "Right. A few days. Where do you want to meet?"

"Tampa General?"

"Give me four hours, I'll see you there."

He disconnected, and Kathryn offered a thumb's up at Marshall. "Four hours."

"It'll be dark."

"I can drive at night. It's an amazing thing."

"Ha, ha. I said I wanted to meet him before I leave

Jackie in his care. We have two hours to interview Richard."

"Jackie's expecting someone to meet her at the coffee house."

"If you pick her up, I can tell Richard she's on her way out of town. I want to drop in on Hayes before we go. Meet me there," he checked his watch, "at six o'clock."

"Will do. Are you planning to grab a bite at the hospital, or should we bring you something?"

"Black coffee would not go amiss. Other than that, I'll manage." He stopped in front of her, less than a foot of space between them.

Kathryn wanted to ignore his wide shoulders, but found his hazel eyes glittering with something that made her want to close the gap. "You should get going."

"I'm working on it."

"We should work harder. This attraction is not good for us."

"You started it."

"So, I should end it."

"You haven't moved yet."

With a sigh, Kathryn forced herself to lower her eyes and turn toward the street. But Marshall slipped an arm around her shoulders, pulled her around, and they were kissing. When they finally pulled apart, she had to blink to focus. "What did you do that for?"

"Just in case." His thumb moved against her cheek. Kathryn felt it all the way to her toes.

She gripped the leather strap of her purse and walked to her jeep. Concern for Lizzie and the need to solve the case warred against the buzz she felt from

Marshall's arms, from the warmth of his kiss.

~

He shouldn't have, but he did. Marshall grinned. He waited for Kathryn to get in her vehicle. The woman seriously threatened to his bland world. He needed to talk to Richard and check on Hayes. She pulled away, and he turned to do his job.

Marshall went to Richard when he returned to the station, but the older man hunched in his chair, arms crossed, chin tucked. He refused to speak, insisting on a lawyer. Marshall had no choice but to leave him alone in the cold room. He went to his office instead. The massive desk reminded him of meeting Kathryn. There were reports in the wire basket, but nothing about either of the bodies. Marshall dropped them back into the baskets.

If Richard wasn't talking, maybe he could check on Hayes early. They didn't need to leave for Tampa for another hour or so. When he arrived, Hayes seemed agitated. Marshall stood just outside the door. The stern look on Hayes face was dark, menacing. Anger posed a real reaction to being shot. Marshall pushed away memories of his own experience, knocked on the door, and entered the room. The odd look vanished, to be replaced by Hayes' usual friendly countenance. Marshall didn't let it fool him. "Have they had you talk with a shrink yet?"

"Sir?"

"Standard procedure after getting shot. Gives you a chance to talk through anger and anything else you may be feeling."

"I'm not feeling angry."

"I've been where you are. Anger is a natural result,

toward yourself. Toward the man who shot you."

"Brenda says you brought Richard in."

"Brenda, huh?" Marshall teased, enjoying Hayes twitching smile. Marshall tapped the moveable table beside the hospital bed. "Looks like she brought you something better than dull hospital food."

"A burger from Beef O'Brady's." He rubbed his stomach. "She may be a saint."

"Can't argue with you there. She does her best to watch out for all of us. How are you feeling today?"

"Like I've been shot. And given enough morphine to take the edge off a cliff."

"Don't get hooked on the stuff." Marshall pointed at the drip machine. "I need you back as soon as possible."

"Sounds like that woman is helping out."

"Kathryn will hang around until she knows her sister is safe."

"I thought someone murdered her sister."

"She's in a coma."

"Here?"

Marshall shook his head. "Hospital in Tampa."

"You found her?"

"Not officially. We're concerned whoever is killing the gang will want to finish the job. We want to keep her safe until this is solved and over."

"What's Richard got to say?"

"Nothing. He's scared of someone. I think they threatened Jackie."

"That old woman? Whatever for?"

"To keep him quiet. Kathryn has an idea to get Jackie out of the way safely. If we can show Richard his mom's safe, maybe he'll explain what's going on.

Why would a gang of thieves come all this way and start killing each other?"

"No honor among thieves?"

"I thought it was the other way around."

"Only if their corporal is Robin Hood."

Marshall laughed. "I doubt these guys are planning to help the poor." Hayes' eyes drifted close then popped open again. Marshall grinned. "Morphine's working, huh? I'll let you rest. For now. I'll check with the doctor about when to expect you to return to duty."

"I'll shoot for Monday, at least give me a weekend to rest."

"I think the city of Dalton will survive until then."

The meeting had taken little time. Marshall found his way to the cafeteria, positioned himself with a view of the street, and settled in with the newspaper and a plate of cheese fries.

~

"Have you been in the sun, dear? Your face is flush." Jackie greeted Kathryn, hugged her, and then pulled back. "Don't they make you wear sunblock?"

Kathryn smiled. "I try to remember. How are you?"

"Ready for a hot cup of tea. I like mine with milk and honey." She tapped the display with a delighted groan. "I'll take one of those cinnamon scones. Should I nab a table in the back or by the window?"

"Somewhere in the middle is fine." Kathryn moved to the counter. A cooler with ice cream stood to her right, which explained why a coffee shop would be open after four. She ordered Jackie's tea, although the lady behind the counter already knew how she liked it. The pastries didn't appeal to Kathryn. "I'll have a double scoop of coffee chip and a water."

"I'll bring it over to the table for you. Here," she handed Kathryn an oversized magazine, "these just came in. Jackie enjoys news around town."

Kathryn grinned. "I can see that." An image of an old house filled the cover of the local periodical. Several artists stood in front. One had a large painting leaning against her leg. A man held his arm around a sculpture that resembled junk more than anything. Kathryn took the chair across from Jackie and placed the magazine on the table. "What do you think this is?"

Jackie turned it around to look. "Maggie's house? I heard she opened it to a variety of artists when Al passed. There's a gallery upstairs now that Maggie's moved into an assisted living community in Tampa."

"Are there a lot of artists in the area?"

"Not like Key West, but I think we have a growing niche for them here."

"No wonder Lizzie liked this place."

The waitress brought a tray with their order. Kathryn sighed at the sweet taste of coffee ice cream. It should be good enough to erase the taste of Marshall's kiss.

Jackie pulled her muffin apart. "What do you think of our city?"

"Never stayed anywhere this small, at least not that I remember."

"Small?" Jackie chuckled. "Drive a little further east, you'll find places like Lake Wales and Yeehaw Junction. Now *those* are small."

"I've spent the past few years in big cities."

"I'm sorry, hon," Jackie patted Kathryn's hand. "You'll get over it, I'm sure."

They chatted a bit longer. When Kathryn checked

the time, it was after five already. She stood. "We're going to stop by the hospital to get Marshall."

"There's a good man in need of a woman."

"I think he's more concerned with solving cases and protecting your community."

"A police officer's job may be more than the average nine to five, but they still need a life. You know that, don't you?"

Kathryn scraped the bottom of her bowl for the last of the ice cream. "I haven't had a life in the past two years, not since working undercover. It eats up everything."

"Will you go back to that job once we finish here?"

"Not that one. I broke my trust by leaving. It'd be too risky to go back."

"Maybe it's time to try somewhere a bit smaller than Miami. A bit slower?"

Kathryn smiled collecting their trash. "You aren't subtle, are you?"

"Never been a quality I admired."

"Do you want this?" Kathryn reached for the magazine.

"Oh, I'll stick that in my bag." Jackie plopped her oversized gray purse on the table. Kathryn wasn't sure what all she kept in that thing, but it could prove useful.

Kathryn sent a text letting Marshall know they were on their way after nabbing him a black coffee. She picked a blueberry muffin for him as well. Jackie paused in front of the jeep when they left the coffee shop. "You have a big gun and a big car."

"This baby belonged to my aunt. She gave it to me. I've had the engine rebuilt, but otherwise, it's been more trustworthy than any of the people I know."

Jackie squeezed Kathryn's hand before getting into the car. "You don't know the right people."

"Probably true. Here, hold this. It's for Marshall." Kathryn handed her the coffee and pastry bag once Jackie settled and buckled herself in. Kathryn walked around to the driver side. Would the right sort of people prove trustworthy? Could Marshall? The thought of relying on him made her insides swirl, but was it a good feeling or fear? She shook the unsettled thoughts. Instead, she got in and started the car.

The drive to the hospital didn't take long. Marshall slipped into the back. He accepted the coffee but groaned at the muffin. "With this and cheese fries for dinner, I'm running a few extra miles tonight."

"Kathryn had scoops of ice cream," Jackie shared. "She should probably join you."

"I think getting us to Tampa and settled will be the highlight of my evening. Besides, why run if nothing's chasing you?"

"How do you keep in shape?" Marshall asked. "Oh, turn here. You'll stay on sixty to County Line Road then cross to I-4."

"The place I stayed in Miami has those Peloton bikes. Got good at spin class."

Jackie turned slightly in her seat. "We have a stretch group that meets in the park weekday mornings. That's the closest I get to exercise."

They passed through another small town before reaching County Line.

"How's that officer doing?" Jackie asked.

"Hayes? He's sore."

"You'll make sure to get the whole story?"

"I've tried to convince Richard to talk, but your son

is stubborn. Does he get that from you or his dad?"

"Hayward could be stubborn when he wanted something." Jackie smiled.

"How long were you married?" Kathryn interjected, shooting a look at Marshall through the rearview mirror. Talking about a suspect with his mother wasn't standard procedure.

"Thirty-two years. You know, I was almost forty-two when we got married. Why, I felt like the Biblical Sara having that boy at my age."

Kathryn laughed. "Did it make you feel younger or older?"

"Blessed." She looked at Marshall. "I know he's not done right, but this will change him, for the better."

"He loves you, very much. That says something about him."

They quieted while Kathryn pulled into the stream of traffic on I-4. She honked at another car cutting in front of her. "If this turns into a parking lot, I may use my siren and drive the shoulder."

"Growth is good for the state, but it does challenge our infrastructure."

Traffic continued to flow, and Kathryn followed Marshall's directions to the hospital. She pulled around the back to park.

Jackie unhooked her seatbelt. "You make a fine team."

Marshall laughed. "We're both well-trained."

~

Marshall let the ladies walk ahead of him. He checked the parking lot. The tingling feel of being watched was back, but nothing moved. No suspicious persons waited in the periphery. The doors of the hospital whooshed open, sending the scent of disinfectant over them. It always brought to mind waking up in a hospital bed, monitors beeping, his dad asleep in a chair near the window. He buried the memory and focused on the lobby, then he had to cover a chuckle. For an undercover cop, JD stood out in a crowd. Marshall glanced at Kathryn. Her eyes lit with recognition, and she smiled at the tall stranger in a way that made him want to hit something. At least he couldn't doubt the man's ability to protect.

Jackie giggled. "Looks like a cross between Dwayne Johnson and Bruce Willis."

"Hopefully, he's got brains to go with the brawn."

Jackie gave him a look. "You think she would trust anyone but the best with her sister?"

"I'm sure they make the power duo."

Jackie's smile widened. "She trusts him with her sister, but she trusts you with herself."

Kathryn reached the stranger then led him toward Marshall and Jackie. "This is Sergeant Franklin. He's in charge of the investigation. This is Jackie." Kathryn introduced.

"Must be a special man to pull this one off the streets. JD," the stranger said, offering his hand to Marshall.

"It's her sister's doing, but I'm glad she's here." Marshall matched JD's tight handshake.

"And calling me to babysit. I can see this one will give me a run for my money." He grinned, shaking Jackie's hand.

"Handsome with a bit of sass?" Jackie tilted her head. "I bet you're a lady's man."

"Gonna make me work at charming you, huh?"

“Enough, both of you.” Kathryn shook her head. “The hospital moved Hope to the courtyard side. You’ll have a suite in the hotel across the way with direct view of Hope’s room. It’s not the most exciting thing in the world, but the idea is to stay safe. JD has a job on the floor at the hospital. Jackie, you binge watch whatever you want. No calls to any of your friends in Dalton. Or anywhere.” Kathryn added for good measure.

“We want you and Hope to stay safe,” Marshall said, giving JD a hard look.

The other man smiled. “I’ve got this. If trouble comes, there’s another safehouse already set. Who’s Hope?”

“My sister.”

“Sister? I didn’t know you had any family.”

“Not the sort of job to broadcast personal matters. She’s in a medically induced coma. I don’t know how long they’ll keep her that way. When she wakes up, let me know.”

“I will.”

Kathryn breathed. “She’s got answers to a lot of questions.”

Marshall resisted the urge to wrap his arm around her stiff shoulders. This Kathryn held herself closed off, focused on business. JD didn’t seem surprised. Marshall rubbed his hand over the back of his neck. “Give me your keys and I’ll grab Jackie’s bag from the back of the SUV. We can walk across the courtyard to the hotel.”

~

Kathryn nodded. She barely looked at him as she dropped the key fob in his hand.

“Should you help?” Jackie asked.

"He seems capable." JD pointed at a shop instead. "I'm sure hours of TV isn't your favorite way to spend a day. What say we find some puzzles or games?"

"A juicy mystery?" Jackie brightened. "I also enjoy a good crossword. How about you?" She asked Kathryn.

"I'll wait for Marshall." She waved them off. They left her alone and the pressure across her shoulders slackened. JD was a good cop. A good man. She shouldn't feel cold around him. Marshall didn't make her cold. He made things a little too heated. Speaking of which, she turned and saw him entering the lobby. There was no reason why she should be that aware of him.

"Lost them already?" He teased, one end of his mouth forming a half-smile.

"He offered to get Jackie some distractions."

"How long have you known him?"

"The few years we've been in Miami."

"But he didn't know you have a sister?"

"You don't know much about me either."

"It's only been a few days. Give me time."

She wanted to. For the first time in her life she wanted to share the nightmare of childhood. Share the fears that kept her from meaningful relationships. She clamped down her emotions. "I've got to get back to my job in Miami, eventually. Not much time to give you." JD and Jackie were walking back with an additional bag. Kathryn pulled on her purse strap. "The door into the courtyard is this way." She led them.

There were grassy paths and cement squares with large flowerpots filled with a variety of chrysanthemums for late fall. A fountain gurgled in the middle. The hotel side of the courtyard had benches and an area of chairs and tables around a bistro kiosk. When they approached the automatic doors, they slid open.

Jackie gasped. "I can't complain about not being held in style." The glitz of chrome and gleaming wood marked the lobby of the familiar chain.

"Let me grab your keys." Kathryn set off for registration. Marshall joined her. She tightened her hold on the purse. "You didn't have to—"

"Give them time to bond. I want to be sure Jackie is comfortable staying in his care."

Kathryn relaxed. "Makes sense."

"Where do we go from here?"

"Home for a good night's sleep."

He grinned. "I'm not going to touch that."

The gleam in his eye caused heat to infuse her cheeks. Drat the man. She rolled her eyes. "You wish. Have you seen your latest local magazine? Jackie picked one up at the coffee shop."

"Am I in it?"

"The cover story is about an artist colony. We haven't found materials at the house. Maybe Lizzie set up a craft space somewhere else. Someplace like the one in the magazine. How many of them can there be in Dalton?"

Marshall rubbed his chin. "Tomorrow's Sunday. We won't find out much, but it's a lead."

A woman with Asian features waved them over. "Welcome," she greeted. "Do you have a reservation?"

"Yes, ma'am," Kathryn's voice took on a southern accent. "Baker. Judith Baker. This is my husband, Jethro."

"Ah, yes, Mrs. Baker. I have a suite overlooking the

courtyard. I'll just need a credit card for incidentals."

Marshall reached for his wallet, but Kathryn placed her hand on his arm and gave a sweet smile. "My treat, remember?" She pulled a card from a slot in the back of her purse and handed it over. "Think it'll be warm enough for the pool tomorrow?"

The receptionist nodded. "It's Florida. It'll be warm enough through mid-November." She ran the card then handed it back with a small envelope. "Here are your keys. Enjoy your stay."

"Thank you, we will." Marshall chuckled as they walked away. "I'm a lowly detective," he muttered. "Espionage may take a while to master."

"You did great. Although, trying to use your own credit card would have spoiled the secret." She couldn't keep herself from teasing him.

They returned to JD and Jackie. Both seemed comfortable with the other. Kathryn handed JD the keys. "No need for us to go up. The card on file will take care of meals. You can text me an update, especially if anything happens with Hope."

"Are you good?" Marshall asked Jackie.

"I'll be fine." Jackie wrapped her arm around JD's. "Tell Richie it's time to do the right thing." She looked at JD. "Lead on, young man."

Kathryn and Marshall watched them walk to the elevators. "Did you want to stop in on your sister?"

"I shouldn't." They went out of the hotel into the courtyard. All that remained of the day was a soft glow in the west.

"There's no reason not to. I'd like to see how good the view to the hotel is."

"Alright. You have a point."

Neither one felt like talking. The path they walked curved through tropical plants. Lights to mark the way between the hotel and hospital turned on. It felt comfortable, surrounded by warm air with a hint of moisture in the twilight. The sterile chill that greeted them in the hospital tore the comfortable feeling away. Kathryn double-checked the room number with reception. Marshall pushed the elevator button. Kathryn crossed her arms and stiffened her back before they walked into the small room. Lizzie remained the same, a pale figure surrounded by beeping machines. The monitor showed a steady heartbeat. She watched it jump up and down while Marshall went to the window checking on the proximity of the hotel. He seemed satisfied.

"Come on," he wrapped his arm around her shoulders, turning her, then walking out of the room.

She allowed his warmth to soak through some of the chill she felt seeing Lizzie lying lifeless.

"I'll drive back," he offered.

"I'm fine. Nobody drives Baby but me. Not since Auntie died."

"It's dark, and I know the roads better. We'll stop at the hospital where my car is. You know your way from there." He walked to the passenger side of the car, waiting to hold it open for her.

"I'm not giving you the keys."

But he pulled them from his pocket with a wicked grin. She'd never gotten them back when he went for Jackie's bag. "Fine. Put a scratch on her and I'll break your finger."

He laughed. "I could say the same about you driving my SUV. I think we'll have to trust each other, at least when it comes to vehicles."

His hand on her arm sometime later nearly caused her to jump out of her skin. "Here's my car. You know where you're going?"

She blinked. The time had changed by at least an hour. "Yeah, I got it from here." They both got out. Kathryn chided herself. Falling asleep? What was this man doing to her? How much deeper would she fall if it took more than a few days to wrap up the case? "I'll talk to you tomorrow," she said when their path's crossed. She did wait to make sure his Escalade started before heading towards Lizzie's house.

Chapter 12

"Sir? We have a report of a body out on Lake Shore Drive. Couple of fishermen just called it in." Brenda broke into his peaceful morning.

Marshall rested his head against the steering wheel, having started the car with the hopes of heading to the station to convince Richard his mother was safe. Now, this would take precedence. "Did you contact the medical examiner's office?"

"I wanted to let you know first."

"Give Allen a call. Tell him to alert the crew. I'll send exact coordinates when I get there. What about Brussels? Has she shown up at the station yet?"

"I haven't seen her, sir."

"Contact her, too. Tell her I'll be in as soon as I can. If she can type the reports for Animal Lodge and the shelter, I'd be even more grateful."

Brenda chuckled. "I'm sure she'll let you know her thoughts on that regard."

Without a doubt. Did he feel a flicker of anticipation? "I need a hobby."

"Sir?"

"MEs office, Brenda. STAT."

Another body. Not even seven days since Kathryn stalked into the station, since Jackie reported someone being shot in the parking lot. A few miles east of town, he turned onto the lake road. Scrub fields grew on either side of the two-lane paved road. A ridge lined with pines stood to the northwest, while blue shimmered in the other direction. He headed toward the water.

Pavement gave way to a dirt lane with deep ruts. The SUV bounced as he drove along the water's edge trail. A pair of brown waving arms drew him to the side of the path. An elderly Mexican and a younger man stood beside their simple motor fishing boat. The elder held his hat in his hands and sent uncomfortable glances to the left. The young man kept his eyes fixed on the ground.

"Good morning." Marshall greeted after stepping from the vehicle.

The elder shook his head. "Not good morning."

No, it wouldn't be. "Why don't you tell me what happened?"

"My grandson and I came early to fish. We have three bites this little time."

"Did you find the body in the water?"

He shook his head. "On the edge. His blue jacket I see."

"Have you fished here before?"

Both men nodded.

"Anything unusual? Did you see anyone?"

"We saw nothing. This one," he jerked his head toward the mound not far away. "He is here longer than today."

"Let me call the station, and then I'll get your contact information."

Though obviously reluctant, the older man provided the necessary information. Marshall heard vehicles on the road before he'd completed the digital form. This time, Marshall found himself beside a bloated body, holding a hankie against his mouth and nose. The cool October morning helped keep stench from wafting through the air, but the process of decay could not be stopped.

"A real floater, this one." Allen seemed too pleased with the discovery.

"How old is it?"

"Age? Or are you talking time of death?" The skinny man laughed at his own joke. "He spent a few days in the water. Fed a few fish and bottom dwellers. This one will be harder to identify. Don't think we'll get any prints from him."

"Work your magic, Doc. Is he about the same age as the alley man?"

Allen nodded. "Same tattoo on his neck."

"I'll walk the perimeter of the lake."

Eagle Lake spread toward the horizon. A trail led along the edge. The tangle of scrub on either side looked undisturbed. Though cold had yet to settle across central Florida, brown and tans stood out among fading green strips. His feet crunched along the broken shell and stone path. Murmuring voices faded behind him. The stillness of morning wrapped peacefully around him. Songbirds garbled, flying between the trees and the fields. Water lapped along the edge. Cattails knocked against each other. It would be a pleasant walk if he wasn't searching for evidence of murder.

A random cloud breached the sun, and a shadow fell across the path. Marshall felt a chill against his back. Someone watched him. The trees along the ridge offered shadows for hiding. He continued along the path but kept his attention in the distance. Was that movement? Something had shifted.

A shot spit dust into the air a short distance ahead of him. The retort startled fowl along the shore, and a gaggle rose with loud protest and took to the air. Marshall dove to his belly, taking cover in the brush. He pulled his phone from his pocket and pressed the station number.

"Give me Brussels," he barked at Brenda. A moment later, Kathryn's familiar voice filled his ear.

"Where are you? We were interrogating Richard this morning."

"Your jeep working?"

"Of course. What does that—"

"Get directions to Eagle Lake from Brenda. We've got a second body and unfriendly fire. Call me when you hit the dirt road and I'll lead you in."

"Don't get shot." She hung up.

He didn't intend to. He flopped onto his stomach and surveyed the area. Something red hid among the weeds. He crawled forward using his forearms. Burrs scraped against his skin from a prickly bush among the other brush. He pushed it out of the way. A red sneaker lay on its side. Mud had caked along the heel. From a body being dragged? He sat cautiously, unwilling to make himself a target. Nothing stirred, and the cold sense of being watched faded away. From his vantage point, markings in the dirt and through the brush led to the water's edge.

His pocket vibrated.

~

"They dragged him through here." He showed Kathryn the mark of shoes in the dirt. They followed the marks and found a larger, disturbed area.

"He was alive here." Kathryn shaded her eyes, looking toward the lake.

Marshall should be observing the distance himself, but her soft checkered shirt drew his attention. "What kind of woman wears plaid?"

She looked at him. "The kind that didn't bring a jacket for the slight chill in the morning air. How many shots did you hear?"

Back to work. "One. Someone intended for me to find this. The murderers incapacitated the victim here and dragged him to the water."

"Do we know how he was killed?"

"Allen will call once he has something definite. This is connected to the murder in the alley." He tapped his neck. "They both had similar tattoos."

"A falling out among thieves?"

"The last man standing gets the pot."

"That means at least two of them are feeling real nervous by now." Kathryn crouched and opened the camera bag. She pulled tags and handed them to Marshall. They worked together placing markers and photographing the scene.

"There should be a ruler in the side. Use it across the width of the trail and the shoe."

They completed the task and followed the trail to the water. Marshall knelt beside a patch of broken stalks. "No sign of a struggle. He must have been killed back there."

"What then? They weigh him down and toss him in?"

"And a few days later he rises to the surface for fishermen to find."

"Who died first? The alley man or him?"

"The man in the alley was less than 24 hours, killed early Tuesday morning. This body's been a couple of days. He may have been killed before the guy in the alley."

"Or he may have helped with the break-ins."

"We wouldn't be able to tell." He rubbed his fingertips. "No usable prints."

"Why lead you here in the first place? How does this help them?"

"Doesn't make sense unless they're taunting us."

"I don't think they'd hide here and reveal themselves. Not if they can help it."

"A vigilante? Someone knows their secret and is trying to dole out judgment?"

"Like you say, doesn't make sense."

"We need to talk with Richard. He has to have a few answers."

Chapter 13

The police interview room included a small square table with carved ruts across the top. The wood chairs were slightly more comfortable than metal ones. Richard looked uncomfortable, fidgeting in the metal seat across from Marshall. A bland-looking young man with light brown hair sat beside Richard. Marshall leaned back, his right ankle atop his left knee. Kathryn grinned at the image of opposites the two of them posed.

"I never meant to hurt a police officer. You have to believe me." Richard leaned forward, then tilted to the side, trying to cross his legs. He changed his mind and scooted his chair closer to the table.

"You've got a lot of explaining to do. Find a beginning."

Richard looked at his lawyer, who nodded. "Wes and me were drinking buddies." He glanced at the clock. "I met him at the pub. He'd get quiet a few times, down about something. But I don't know what. He never told me."

"What happened the night the girl got shot?"

"I can't believe Mom witnessed it. Of all the dumb luck. Wes came to my house but got called away. This other guy, I've seen him before. I guess he called Wes' girl. He wanted to get something from her. Mom ran back. When I got down there, Wes's crying, leaning over her and pressing his shirt against her side. The other guy shouts and waves his gun. Wes told him to get out of there. I told Wes to get her to the hospital. He didn't want to go local, so I suggested Tampa Memorial. But he'd have to hurry. We got her onto the backseat of his car. I used the shirt to clean up the ground. There wasn't much."

"Where did you put the shirt?"

"Dumped it on my way to work."

"Did he make Tampa?"

He shrugged. "Don't know. Never heard from him."

"Why shoot Hayes?"

His arms crossed and uncrossed and he chewed his bottom lip. Very uncomfortable, but why?

"I received a letter. They threatened Mom as well as me."

"Just a letter? That's all?"

He shook his head.

"What else?"

He leaned forward, a muscle in his cheek ticking. "A finger. There was a bloody finger in the envelope. When that knock came, I thought it was them."

"What if it had been a girl scout selling cookies? You didn't know who was on the other side of that door."

"I called for help. I wasn't going to let him bleed to death on the stoop."

"That saved his life, but even if we call it an

accidental shooting, you're going to do time."

His shoulders drooped. "Mom'll disown me."

"Not your mom."

"Am I safe here?"

"You better be, or she'll have my hide. Did Wes tell you what they were looking for?"

Richard shifted in his seat again.

"You aren't responsible for their crimes. If you know something—"

"I think he had some jewels. Her, that girl, she got hold of them. Maybe because he liked her, I don't know. She had the jewels and the other guy wanted them back."

"But Lizzie doesn't have them all, because she'd been making dog collars for the local shops."

"Lizzie? Did you find her?"

"No. If Wes headed to Tampa, we'll start searching the roadside."

Marshall exited the interview room. Kathryn remained beside the two-way mirror, hands in her pocket. She watched Richard through the glass. The observatory door rattled, and Marshall entered.

"Do you believe him?" She asked, but at first glance he didn't appear to be thinking about the case. His attention was on her. He shook himself, and his eyes refocused.

"For the most part. I don't like how he latched onto Lizzie's name."

"The body from the river missed a finger?"

He agreed. "I'll get a team to his apartment. See what we can find."

"I received a text from JD while you were…" she motioned with her thumb to the double glass window.

“Good. He thinks they’re safe?”

“And sound.”

“If your sister still has gems, where would she hide them?”

“The robberies occurred after she was shot and one of the perps murdered. Maybe those collars were all she had.”

“Would she know how valuable they are? Could she have thought they were fake?”

“I don’t know. Maybe. Maybe at first. Why does it matter?”

“Puzzle pieces. This isn’t going to make sense until we have all the puzzle pieces.”

“What’s next?”

“I’ll get Richard’s place done tonight. Tomorrow, we’ll search Lizzie’s house more thoroughly. We can run your idea about an artist studio, maybe she rented a space.”

“I’ll order bios from Philadelphia, find out who the other gang members are. It’ll be harder to hide here than in the big city.”

“Want to help at Richard’s?”

She stepped closer. He smelled like coffee. She liked the way his Adam’s apple bobbed. “Won’t be the first time I’ve seen a severed finger.”

The thought dimmed the gleam sparking in his hazel eyes. “It’s probably been flushed.”

Kathryn tilted her head. “Do you have keys to Jackie’s place?”

He frowned. “Why?”

“Richard might have felt safer hiding something at mom’s than his own place.”

“I’ll get a warrant. Let’s go.”

Chapter 14

Kathryn drummed her fingers on the steering wheel looking up at the apartment complex. Richard lived in the last apartment on the right, second floor. There would be an apartment behind his. One on the left, and one underneath. She grabbed a stick of gum, tried to poof her shoulder-length hair, and grabbed the jean jacket from the back seat before leaving the jeep. She crossed the parking lot, but instead of heading upstairs, she went to the apartment under Richard's. She knocked on the door, hoping Sunday afternoon would find someone home.

The door opened to a tall lanky man holding a can of beer. "Ya better not be from no church." He frowned.

"Oh, no. I'm Bobby Jo. Somewhat new, moved upstairs on the other side." Kathryn smacked her gum as she wrapped her words with a deep southern drawl.

"What do ya need? I don't move no furniture."

She giggled. "Already got a man to take care of that

for me. Nah. I just wondered about my neighbor. The one above you. He's got some odd noises coming from his apartment. Makes my little Precious yap something fierce. You can't hear her, can you? I'd feel terrible if you did."

"What do you expect me to do?"

"Nothing. Just wondering if its usual for him to make a lot of noise. You being his downstairs neighbor, well, I figured you'd know best. Me 'en Precious'd have to move."

"Richard's not bad. Don't hear nothin' from him most days. Now, if you can catch his mom when she's here cooking a meal—that's worth a drop-in."

"I am thankful to hear that. Don't you worry none about church people neither. They helping people find the Lord. My grandmama used to take me when I was a little girl. That woman could sing. You ever get to hear your grandmama sing in church?"

He looked down and shuffled his feet. "Well, yeah. Guess I did."

"There you go. Them church people can't all be bad." She winked at him. "I'll see you around." She waved before she wandered off.

Marshall caught up with her in the stairwell. "What are you doing? I asked you to stay put until I had a look around the complex."

"Trying to ascertain if Richard would go to extreme lengths to hide something valuable. Downstairs neighbor is the most likely to know if floors have been forced up or walls broken into."

"I didn't think about that possibility."

"I doubt Richard did either. Freezer and toilets are traditional hiding spots, at least when it comes to drugs."

"The warrant's secure and I've got keys. We can take any technology with us."

The door had a hole from the bullet that got Hayes. Inside, a faint smell of lemon hung in the air. "Cleaner than I thought," Kathryn commented pulling on plastic gloves.

"Jackie's influence. Kitchen or bedroom?"

"I'll take the kitchen. You can explore those mysterious male parts of the house."

Marshall shook his head. "Put it like that, maybe you should go back there."

Kathryn ignored him. She walked into the galley kitchen with builder grade cabinets and solid surface counter in gray. The floor tiles were darker gray and appliances modern stainless steel, also builder-grade. The side-by-side refrigerator fit into a surround of cabinets. It didn't have water or ice dispenser in the door. She opened the freezer side. Someone made sure Richard had his vegetables. She started at the top rack, checked each of the boxes for tampering. Tupperware dishes had soup or spaghetti sauce clearly labeled with dates. The bucket of ice was full. She laid a towel over the drain in the sink and dumped the ice. There seemed to be nothing but frozen water. She methodically went through each of the other shelves and the two bins at the bottom. She closed the door and rubbed her arms before continuing the refrigerator side. Nothing suspect showed up. She moved to the far end of the galley kitchen and started searching cabinets.

Marshall joined her. She opened the third lower cabinet to the right of the sink. "The back bedrooms and hall both look clear."

"Same here. I've got the ice melting in the sink, but it all looks wet." She stood. "No sign of a letter or finger?"

"Nothing. Why get rid of them?"

"Probably thought he'd be in trouble for helping get rid of a body."

"Or he lied and never received a letter."

Kathryn moved to the next cabinet beneath the sink. "I thought you said he seemed genuinely concerned for Jackie."

"He's scared." Marshall agreed. "I wonder if fear is keeping him from telling us all the truth."

"Let's finish up here and look at Jackie's. Tomorrow, we'll see if we can find the art studio where Lizzie worked."

"Yes, sir," Marshall saluted with a smile.

Kathryn took a breath. "Little pushy for someone who doesn't really work here?"

"A little."

They finished with the apartment. The drive to Jackie's took less than ten minutes. Jackie's house, although older, had a charm making it more inviting than Richard's apartment. Photos on the wall presented captured moments. Proved the family knew laughter. An older couple doting on their only child. Unease made her rub her hands on her jeans. What if her childhood had been different?

"Did you find something?" Marshall asked.

"What?" Kathryn turned. "No. Spying on a family feels awkward."

"How about you take bedroom duty and I'll start in the kitchen? Not sure I'm ready for old lady secrets.

Kathryn rolled her eyes. "Coward."

"I call it smart."

Kathryn didn't mind Jackie's room. Walking across the thick plum carpet reminded her of the woman. Plenty of light flooded through three windows. The queen-sized bed had a white bedspread. The walls were painted soft blue. A large frame beside the bed had a picture of her husband smiling. Kathryn checked the dresser and the small closet. Older homes, she shook her head.

On one wall stood a tall jewelry case with eight drawers and two sides that opened to hold necklaces. A few of the pieces looked real, but no loose stones. She checked the bathroom. Pulling the top from the toilet back, she found something taped inside. Before removing the package, she pulled her phone from her pocket and took a few pictures. The duct tape pulled away easily. Kathryn held a Ziploc bag, folded into quarters, with something inside. She went in search of Marshall. "I found something."

~

Marshall turned at Kathryn's declaration. She hurried into the dining room. She put something on the table, snapped a picture with her phone, then unfolded a package.

"Is that drugs?"

"No, it's paper." She laid it flat and took another picture. "Thin, like ordinary printer paper."

"You found it in Jackie's room?"

"Taped underneath the toilet lid."

He shook his head, admiring her for a moment. "You called it." Her eyes scooted away from his, causing him to grin.

"Franklin, get your mind on task." She berated.

"You're a distraction."

"I can leave if it will help."

"You're too curious to see what's on the paper to leave."

Her lips twitched as she met his gaze. "Didn't say I wouldn't take the package with me if I leave."

He rolled his eyes. "Fine. Pull the paper out nice and easy. Let's make sure there's nothing between if there's more than one page."

She took a breath, then continued removing the paper from the bag. "I see three sheets. Let me turn this top one over."

The grainy image showed several men. Two in the foreground were clearest. Marshall tapped the face on the left. "Looks like alley man, first body we found."

"Could this be the one from the lake?" Kathryn touched the other.

"No, his hair's too different. There's someone in the background, but I can't tell anything about him."

"Are you sure it's a him?" She squinted, turned the paper to the side, but shrugged. She turned over the other two pictures. There were slight variances. Though additional people could be seen in the background, the details were too distorted to recognize anyone. Kathryn stacked the papers and returned them to the baggie. "The quality isn't high. Cell phone maybe?"

Marshall pulled an evidence bag from the case they brought with them. "We dumped the phone Richard had. There weren't any pictures like this on it."

"Does Jackie have a phone?"

"She didn't take these." Marshall was certain.

Kathryn looked at him with her hands on her hips. "They were found in her house."

He stepped closer. “I know you haven’t known her long, but I think you read people well. Do you really think Jackie has anything to do with these pictures? Or the situation Richard is in?”

“No.”

“Maybe junior had a different phone, something throwaway to keep in communication with the others.”

Kathryn dropped the baggie into the evidence bag. Marshall pulled the tab to tape it shut, and then filled in the front data sheet. She shook her head. “I don’t think Richard is involved, not directly with the gang. He’s scared, like he learned something and thought he could use it to his advantage.”

“That almost makes sense.” Marshall agreed.

“If Richard stashed these here, he may have printed them here. A forensic technician could retrieve the files.”

“Which means we need to take any computer equipment and printers.”

“Do you have an evidence bag that big?”

He gave her an exasperated tilt of his head. “I’ve got boxes in the back of the Escalade.”

“Useful.”

“We don’t have any local resources for this. I’ll have to check with Tampa or Orlando. Surely one of them can process the equipment.” Marshall went to the SUV and pulled three flats that would fold into boxes. They used two, managing to seal both. Marshall signed and dated the tape. “Results could take a month or longer.” He sighed. He hoped to have the case wrapped up sooner.

Kathryn stepped next to him to help place the boxes in the back of the SUV. Maybe dragging the case a month or more would be okay. He closed the hatch. "Are we still looking for an art studio tomorrow?"

"We?" Her eyes had flecks of silver. She stood her ground, wary, but unwilling to back down. Marshall kept one hand on the vehicle where he'd pushed to close the hatch. Seconds ticked. "Why are we still standing here?" she asked without dropping eye contact.

"Have dinner with me tonight."

"I don't think that's a good idea."

"Most of my ideas since you stormed into our jurisdiction haven't been good."

She moved closer. "Are you saying I have an effect on you?"

Then they were kissing. Oh, yes. She influenced his heart. He pulled away but kept his hand cupped around her cheek. "Is that a yes to dinner?"

"This kissing thing has to stop. And don't you dare say I started it." She narrowed her eyes when he opened his mouth to speak.

"Fine. No more kissing until we get to know each other better. Dinner will help with that." He dropped his hand, enjoying the feel of her silky skin. "There's an Italian place downtown, a few blocks from the station. I'll meet you there."

"Six o'clock. I'll do some tourist exploring while you fill out all the lovely red tape. I can walk around downtown."

"It's Sunday. Everything'll be closed."

She smiled. "Good thing I know how to window shop. Don't worry, I'll meet you at six. You have my cell number, so you can probably track where I am anyway."

Chapter 15

Long shadows of late afternoon stretched across the parking lot. Kathryn felt a shiver of awareness along her spine. The hairs of her neck stood. She pulled her smart phone from her pocket and swiped her thumb across the screen. Her ears perked as she located Marshall's number and sent a text.

Help.

She scanned the area. She could make out the darker forms of trees dotting the lot. A few cars remained parked. But where were the people? She could feel them watching her step off the curb. Questions flashed through her mind. Then she heard it. A van door slid open to her right. Where was Marshall?

She reached for her weapon, but the cold touch of steel against her temple stayed her hand.

"I can fire mine a lot faster than it takes you to pull your gun." A man with a deep voice spoke.

She went still.

"Good choice. Move your hands up and away, nice

and easy so you don't end up with a new hole."

"You're making a mistake." She tried to hold onto her phone, but he snatched it away. Her service revolver got pulled from her shoulder holster.

"Mistakes have been made." He agreed with her, although the pressure of the barrel did not lessen. "All along this misadventure. You're the latest in a long line."

"What do you want?"

"Get in the van."

She tensed, pulling away, but he held her firmly.

He dragged her close enough she could smell mint on his breath. "I've got the upper hand. You die here, right now. Or you take your chances with a ride."

She saw three of them. Could there be others? Years of training told her not to get in the van, but the gun against her head posed the greater threat. She took a step forward.

He pushed.

Moments later she sat against the hard wall of the black van with her hands taped together. Duct tape. Not easy to loosen. Two kidnappers remained with her in the back. She couldn't see their faces. Tension aided her awareness. As the vehicle moved, she recognized crossing two sets of train tracks, and from the tone of the wheels at least one real bridge. She wasn't familiar enough with the area to recognize the location, but hopefully she'd get the chance to share it with Marshall.

A sudden stop jolted her to the side and her shoulder struck the floor. She winced. Someone righted her and then yanked her from the van. She stumbled to her knees. Looking around, she noticed the industrial area. A faint tinge of orange zest hung in the air, tickling her nose. Sporadic lights lit the blacktop. She glanced at the man who grabbed her jacket and pulled her to her feet. He wore black with a mask pulled over his face.

"Through that door." A different man spoke, giving her a shove. His voice had an accent, Canadian maybe.

One area of the warehouse lit up with a bulb. Near the dangling light, a single chair had been set. She protested, but he shoved her into the hard, wood seat.

"I'm tired of games, Ms. Brussels." Canadian loomed over her, hands shoved in his pocket. "I don't know what happened to your sister, but I have you. Give me what I want, or I kill you."

"I'm a cop. Do you understand you're setting yourself up for the death penalty?" She looked at the other two men. "All of you."

Canada's hand struck her across her cheek. "I want my merchandise."

She brushed her hair from her face, even though her hands remained taped together. "The only thing I have is one collar. It's in the evidence room at the station. You got everything else when you hit the dog shops."

He leaned closer, but she refused to back away. "Your sister acquired more than what we recovered."

"How did she acquire them?"

Another hit slammed her head back. Pain radiated through her jaw. She moved her chin slowly. Nothing broken, yet. "You want me to figure out where she stashed them?" She glared. "I need to know more about this situation. I don't have a clue."

He paced a few steps and faced her again. "Your sister started flirting with one of my men. The idiot must have showed her the jewels. He wanted to impress her." He placed both hands on the arms of the chair and leaned close. "Do you know what happened to him? I threw him in the drink. I'm not out to impress anyone." He crouched in front of her and reached behind his back.

Kathryn stiffened as he pulled a Glock into view. She suppressed the shudder of fear and concentrated on details that would help her. His hazel eyes had a hard edge. She'd noticed those eyes before. He'd been talking to Oliver Hughes when she and Marshall entered the jewelry store.

He continued talking. "Your sister got killed too, I believe, though we don't know where she's stashed." He rubbed the barrel of the gun against her cheek. "Wes tried to convince me she paid him for them, but they weren't his to give."

"Maybe Wes got rid of the other ones."

"No. He talked quite freely before the end. Didn't like losing his fingers that way. He gave them to her. Let her take them."

"But we've searched the house twice. We haven't found— "

He slammed the pistol against the side of her head. Fingers of consciousness flickered. The chair hit the floor with her in it. Pain radiated through her arm.

Dots of black danced before her eyes, but she saw someone else enter the warehouse. For a moment, she thought Marshall. But a gun discharged and one of the masked men fell to the floor. She blinked, trying to stay awake. Two more shots, maybe more. The man closest to her lay a foot away, his hazel eyes open yet empty.

Blood dripped in her eye and she couldn't raise her hand to wipe it away. The blurry image stood in the light. A familiar figure. She swallowed and tasted blood. It couldn't be.

"Dad?" Emotion crushed over her and she sunk into oblivion.

Chapter 16

Marshall glanced at his phone when a text binged. *Help.* The single word caused air to catch in his throat. Kathryn was in trouble. It didn't matter they'd known each other only days. He cared about this woman and he wanted the opportunity to see where it led. He glanced at his watch. Five-thirty. She'd be downtown, not too far from the restaurant.

"Brenda, get Officer Copeland and Dennis. Have them search Central four blocks, from the old church to the courthouse."

Brenda stood, her hand on the patrol car communicator. "What are they looking for?"

"I think Brussels ran into trouble. Check for her and anything else that looks suspicious."

Although downtown was mainly along Central, alleys and arcades provided thruways to parking and a few off-Central shops. Marshall checked his phone. Nothing else. No response to his asking *where are you.* No response to calls. Her phone went directly to voice mail. He pulled up the locator app. She would kill him if he used it, but she might also thank him if it saved her life. He activated the app. Her phone wasn't on. Not good.

His ear mic buzzed. "We got something, Sergeant," Dennis muttered.

"Location?" he followed their lead. They found a broken phone in a parking lot a block north of where he told Kathryn to meet him for dinner. Marshall rubbed the back of his neck. He surveyed the parking area. Dim streetlamps offered little help.

"Is it hers?" Copeland asked.

"We should be able to find fingerprints to be certain. Bag it and take it in. It's getting too dark out here."

"What do you think happened?" Dennis moved nearer to Marshall. Copeland picked up the remains of the phone.

"Tire marks could be a large vehicle pulling away."

"Maybe trouble followed her from Miami? She worked undercover, didn't she?"

"The case here has enough trouble of its own. They might think she knows something. Lizzie's her sister."

"Which of these shops have security covering the lot? We could get lucky."

Marshall felt like slapping his forehead. Why hadn't he thought of that? "The jewelry store has video monitoring both exits." He pressed the button on his connection with Brenda.

"Yes, boss?" Brenda responded.

"Get Hughes up to his store. We need to see footage for the parking lot out back."

"Okay. I've got Rosie's number as well if he's out

of town."

~

Rosie Hughes was early fifties, well-rounded, with a penchant for velvety jump suits. Today she wore pink, including the ribbon pulling back her platinum blonde curls. She sank on the chair in front of the computer. "What's our little town coming to? This much activity isn't healthy." She tapped a few keys on the keyboard with long, hot-pink nails. "Here we go." She pulled up a live feed of the rear door camera.

"Does your system record?"

She raised one brow. Rosie might look the part of a dingy blonde, she wasn't. "How far back do you want to see?"

Marshall checked his watch. Six-twenty-three. "Let's start an hour ago."

She clicked controls and a time stamp of five twenty-three appeared in the corner. The lot looked the same. Three of the cars were still there. A black van hovered at the far side of the recording. At five thirty-two, it moved, pulling in reverse, then turning out of the parking lot heading left. South.

"Is there any point when we can see a license plate?" Marshall leaned closer to the monitor.

"You think something's wrong with the van?" Dennis asked as Rosie rewound and played the section a second time. The plate had been removed.

"Yeah, I think something's wrong with the van. Can you send me this file?" He handed Rosie a card with his email. Dispatch buzzed. "What is it, Brenda?"

"We have shots fired at the Holt Factory."

"Who called it in?" Marshall ran through the store with Dennis and Copeland following.

"They didn't leave any personal information. Should I send someone to check it out?"

The orange factory was south of town. "I've got Dennis and Copeland with me. We're on our way. Send an EMT and truck from the firehouse just in case."

"Will do." Brenda clicked off.

"Shots fired?" Dennis asked, grabbing the front passenger seat of the Escalade. "Could that be Brussels? Does she carry?"

"She has a weapon. I don't know if she carried it today." Marshall flipped a switch and sirens roared to life. He raced, a wordless prayer filling his head even as his chest ached.

The black van sat at the entry into the offices and storage area of the factory. Marshall doused the sirens. When the sound sliced to a halt, nothing more could be heard. The three officers stormed from the SUV. Marshall waved Dennis and Copeland to the other side of the open door. He motioned to the window. Copeland shook his head. No visibility through there. The two crawled beneath the window, stepping carefully over the gravel. Marshall crouched by the door. He could see a light toward the back left of the large open space. There were bodies on the floor and what looked like a large dining room chair lying on its side. He looked at the other two officers, but they shook their heads. Nothing to see toward the right. Marshall made the signal for cover, and he entered the building, staying low with the wall to his back. Weapon drawn, he scanned the area. Nothing moved. Sirens from EMT sounded in the distance. Dennis and Copeland drew up beside him. "Move slow and keep your attention focused. This place has no cover." Marshall directed.

They moved. Nothing hindered their progress. Marshall checked the first body. There was no pulse and plenty of splatter. He moved on. Kathryn lay on the ground in the knocked-over chair. He recognized the clothes she wore. He forced himself to stay on task, but it was the hardest thing he'd ever done.

Dennis knelt beside the second man, shook his head. Marshall reached Kathryn. Blood caked in her hair, but there was a wrinkle across her forehead.

"Kathryn?" He whispered her name, then he felt her neck for a pulse. A solid beat against his fingers made him want to shout. Her wrists were bound with tape and her torso had been tied to the chair. She groaned. "Hold on, hon. Don't try moving yet." He gently checked her head wound.

"She's alive?" Copeland leaned over, grabbing hold of the chair.

"Did she do this?" Dennis waved at the bodies.

"Her hands are tied, and I don't see a weapon. Get the paramedics. Who's got a knife?"

Copeland pulled a blade from his belt and handed it to Marshall before running back to the entrance. Marshall cut the rope, then reached for her hands. She struggled, trying to knock him away.

"Hey, it's me. It's okay. It's Marshall. You're safe." With his hand pressed against her cheek, she must have recognized him and stilled. The shadow in her eyes when she opened them caused a slow burning anger unlike anything he'd ever experienced. Her eyes remained uneasy, flickering through the warehouse. Moving her head made her groan.

"Don't move. Cavalry's coming," he assured her.

Wheels of a gurney clicked crossing the concrete

floor. Marshall didn't want to get out of the way.

"Let me take care of her, sir," a young man knelt next to Marshall. A second man joined him, and they immobilized her neck and head before lifting her onto the gurney. She looked pale, especially with blood smeared across her face.

"We'll meet you at the hospital," Marshall promised before letting them take her to the ambulance. He rubbed his hands over his eyes.

"What happened here?" Copeland righted the chair.

Marshall buzzed Brenda. "Send the coroner."

Brenda gasped. "Is it Kathryn? Is she…?"

"She's on her way to the hospital. We've got three others who weren't so lucky."

Chapter 17

Marshall felt no love loss for hospitals, but Kathryn's stubborn streak took on new meaning. Foot tapping in an attempt to keep the words in his head from spilling into the room, Marshall stood inside the door of the hospital room. Kathryn, bandage at her temple and arm in a sling, shifted herself into an upright position. Against doctor's orders. And his. God save him from stubborn women. "This is ridiculous. You can barely keep yourself upright."

She glared, but her usually expressive eyes were shuttered. She kept something from him. He could feel it. "We recovered your weapon. No match for the bullets that killed the three men. Who else was there?"

"I don't know. I only saw three. I got knocked out and woke up in the ambulance."

The anguish of finding her on the floor of the warehouse amidst the other bodies had nearly driven him to his knees. He cared. Possibly more than that, but this cold woman refusing to communicate wasn't what he wanted in his life, in a relationship. "What aren't you telling me?" He tried again.

She offered a dry laugh, though it made them both wince. "I have a killer headache."

"Doctor left you meds."

She looked at the small cup holding three pills. He thought she might reach for them, but her hand fisted and remained at her side. "I'll stick to Aleve when I get home."

"You shouldn't be alone. The doctor wanted you to stay tonight."

"No such luck." She pushed herself to her feet and swayed.

He jerked forward, arms reaching.

She held a hand to forestall him. "I need to do this. I can't explain right now, but I have my reasons."

"I should take you to the station."

"But you're going to let me go home."

"Why?"

She looked at him. "Because it's what I want."

"I don't understand you, Kathryn."

"I've got something to figure out. Just me. Your murder cases are solved."

"Solved? Really? I have three more bodies. How does that solve anything?"

Her face hardened. "Your chief should be back soon. He'll help you figure it out."

He went still. Too much like before, too much like the taunts from his fiancé before she left him. Never again. "Thank you for your input, Deputy Brussels. I guess I'm finished." He turned and walked away. White hot anger caused his heart to beat faster. Other emotions wanted to interfere, but he stuck with anger. It allowed him to leave her alone in the hospital room, though it was the last thing he wanted to do.

~

The room spun and Kathryn sank onto a stuffed chair. The look on his face—anger and betrayal—hurt worse than the pounding against her temple. She shouldn't have let him go, but old fears clenched her chest.

Had her mind tricked her? The man's image mocked her confusion. Wide face, roman nose with its crooked bridge, piercing blue eyes like her own. He couldn't have been there. Not her father. The faulty light in the warehouse tricked her.

She pushed herself to stand once more. How would she get home to Lizzie's? How could she have treated Marshall that poorly? She took a step toward the door. Though the room continued to move, she stayed upright. Another step.

Dad was supposed to be locked up in Louisiana. Someone would have contacted her otherwise, wouldn't they?

The rail along the hall helped, offering a modicum of support when the world tilted too much.

A lady wearing a yellow blouse smiled at her from the front desk. "May I help you, dear?"

"I need a cab." She tried a light laugh. "Doc won't let me drive in this condition."

The attendant's eyes clouded with concern, and she ran her finger along a list taped to the desk. "Just a moment."

Time blurred. She found herself in the cab, rolling to a stop in front of Lizzie's place. She looked at her empty hands with a frown. "I don't have…" she looked at the cabbie. “Wait here. I’ve got to get the fare from the house.”

Her door opened, and a man handed a bill to the driver.

She blinked as Marshall offered his hand. She scooted carefully. “I thought you were angry with me.” She managed to get to her feet but swayed as the world tilted. He steadied her with a light touch against her good arm.

“I am. I’m furious with you.” He said it, but he didn’t sound like it. “I also know you’re in no condition to take care of yourself. I decided we’ll fight about it once you’ve recovered.”

“Sporting of you.” She tried to smile but was sure it resembled a grimace.

“Walk.” He commanded. “Before you pass out on the sidewalk and earn another bump.”

“Not chivalrous enough to catch me?” She walked, determined to close the distance between herself and the front door. By the time she reached it, her muddled thoughts refused to direct her hand to open it.

He reached around her and scooped her into his arms. “It isn’t chivalry,” he assured her. “You’re moving at a snail’s pace and I’m out of patience.”

She no longer cared.

Chapter 18

He shouldn't be here, Kathryn told herself through muddled thoughts. Marshall shouldn't be asleep in a rocker in the guest bedroom she used at Lizzie's house. He was supposed to be mad at her. She sighed.

Though night had fallen, light from the hallway illuminated the room. She must have slept for some time. Her head seemed attached, no longer wobbly. There was a vague memory of pills and cool water. She slid a glance at the sleeping sergeant. He slipped her a pain med and she'd gone right out. Well, she had to be honest with herself, she'd been just this side of collapse.

"You want a drink?"

She liked his eyes, warm hazel with a touch of sleep.

"Yes, but I can get it." She started to rise.

"It's a drink, Punk. Easy for me to provide, and not difficult for you to accept." He stood at her side holding a glass of water before she could protest.

"Can I, at least, sit up so I don't get a bath?"

He laughed and placed the water on the nightstand. He helped her sit and placed two pillows behind her back. "Better?"

She accepted the glass and drank sweet water that cooled her dry throat. "I am. Much better."

He pulled the rocker closer and she felt her heart flip.

"You want to tell me what's going on?"

She liked the friendly Marshall, didn't want to lie to him. But no way could she tell him the truth. At least, not the whole truth. She took a breath. "I overreacted." She apologized, hoping to sidetrack him.

His brows rose. "You don't say?"

"You weren't exactly calm, cool, and collected."

"I don't like when people I think I trust lie to me."

"I didn't lie." She met his gaze. "I was nasty, but I didn't lie. I don't know who shot those men. I was out of it by that time. I thought I saw someone familiar."

"Another case?"

"Yeah. But it doesn't make sense. He has nothing to do with this place." She wasn't technically lying. Dad's case file had to be a few inches thick.

"Who was he?"

She shook her head, and grimaced.

He glanced at his watch. "Sun'll be up shortly. Want me to fix breakfast? Get some food into you and then maybe you'll tell me the truth?"

"I'm not lying," she tried to convince him, held his gaze for a moment. "I like my eggs scrambled." *Get out of my room and give me a moment's peace*. She didn't say the words, but his knowing smile irked her even though he complied.

By the time Marshall left, Kathryn felt the slight twinge of pain in her temple begin to pound harder. Partial truths were lies. She knew it, believed it, and yet that knowledge hadn't prompted her to give him the truth.

She sat at her desk. “Lord, please don't let this be.” The number for the Louisiana prison had imprinted itself on her brain. She dialed, tapping her finger on the gleaming surface while she waited. A few buttons further, and she connected with an Officer Ryan.

“I'm a deputy with the Miami Police Department.” She repeated her name and position a third time.

“You have Wainwright?”

“No. I’m hoping to locate him.”

“As are we.”

“Excuse me?”

“If you read the posts, you should have noticed he was unintentionally released. Traded identity with another inmate.”

“You didn't think to connect with his family? He’s not exactly endeared to them.”

“Has he done something?”

Kathryn rubbed her eyes. “I believed he killed three men who were attempting to harm his daughter.”

“Not a good day to be a bully on the playground when he's in town.”

“I'm glad you can make light.” She paused. “I'm sorry, that was uncalled for. “

“You said he's in Miami?”

“Further north, close to Orlando.”

“I can send someone from the Marshall's office.”

"I already have a Marshall." The pun brought a smile to her face. She'd have to tell him now, with too much at stake. What if Dad found Lizzie? What if he crossed paths with her again? "Thanks for your help. If I get something concrete, I'll give you a call." Her hand shook when she dropped her cell on the desk. Not a trick of her mind. Marshall's voice sounded from the hallway even though she couldn't understand what he said. The thought of food made her stomach flip unpleasantly.

During a slow walk down the stairs, her mind swirled. What to tell? How to tell? What would he think of a woman with that sort of father? The last thought made her head hurt worse.

Marshall offered her a plate with scrambled eggs and toast when she turned into the kitchen. "No bacon."

She reached for the coffee. "My morning runs on coffee."

He pushed the scrabbled egg plate an inch closer to her. "Real food will help with your recovery."

"More sleep will help with my recovery." She looked through the window at the growing dawn. Could he be out there, watching?

"What about telling me what really happened?"

"I already did," Kathryn frowned. Would he be safer not knowing more?

He didn't respond, but his eyes darkened. Any sense of concern for her withdrew from his gaze.

She bit her lower lip. "I'm exhausted. If I remember something more, I'll call. I promise."

"I'll have Officer Copeland connect with you this afternoon to take your statement." He moved toward the living room.

"I'll drop by the office."

"Wait for his call. He'll let you know when he's available."

Marshall left. It was too late to say anything about Wainwright. The pounding in her head doubled. He'd placed the pharmacy bottle with painkillers next to her coffee. Kathryn didn't think, she popped a pill and headed back upstairs.

~

A few hours did wonders. Kathryn stretched, appreciating movement with minimal pain. Her window was filled with light. She glanced at her watch. Nearly noon. The confusion of the morning made her shake her head. Ridiculous. Of course, Sargent Franklin needed to know Wainwright lurked around the small Central Florida town. A few minutes later, door into the garage open, she realized the problem. Her jeep was parked downtown. She called Marshall.

"What?" He barked after the third ring.

"Hey, it's me." Kathryn twirled her hair. Marshall sounded grumpy. Or groggy. He couldn't have gotten much sleep last night in the chair.

"Why?"

Nice. Single word. Choppy. "Um, I wondered if you could take me to get my jeep."

"Brenda can help you."

"Oh. Good, that's fine. Everything alright there?"

"Lots of paperwork. Five bodies make a mess."

"Can I help?"

"I think you've done enough. Call the switchboard and Brenda will answer."

He hung up. Kathryn looked at her phone. What happened to the man who fixed breakfast in order to wheedle information out of her?

"You weren't too pleasant yesterday. Maybe he's returning the favor." The sound of her voice encouraged her. She contacted Brenda and made the necessary arrangements.

Chapter 19

Kathryn's smile faded as Brenda drove away. Standing beside the jeep in the parking lot near the Italian restaurant, thoughts of what she should do evaporated like mists. Her training evaporated like mists. The feel of her pulse racing and the shallow breaths that made it hard to focus- she recognized signs of fear. Fear of Wainwright. Fear of what he had done and could do. He was somewhere, closer than she wanted. Marshall was busy or didn't want to see her. Probably both. She needed to talk with him, explain, but he wouldn't listen until he recovered from their spat. What to do in the interim? Brenda suggested walking downtown, absorb the small-town charm. She forced herself to take a deep breath, hold for ten, and then release. The prisoner needed to be recovered. If she could manage it, walk with him handcuffed into the police station, Marshall would have to listen.

Brenda's idea to explore downtown could work. Might be the only way she'd catch a glimpse of her father. Thinking about the relationship made her skin crawl. Wainwright. “Paul.” Her lip curled at the sound of his name. She peered down Central. The front pillars of the station house were visible, next door to the arched front and steeple of an old stone church. Her thoughts turned toward God. A moment to seek refuge, if only to allow time for the mind-spinning to slow and her usual instinct to save the day. How long had it been since she’d stepped into a church? Undercover work made it impossible. With a sigh, she allowed the thought to slip away. Take her time walking up and down the alleys with stores, and Marshall would be calm enough to reason. If not, perhaps then she’d sit in the church. With hands in her pocket, she began to walk window to window, using reflections to keep watch, observing through veiled lids as she crossed brick-paved paths. But it wasn’t enough.

“Hello, Kathryn.”

The voice immobilized her. He’d found a blind spot, and now hovered behind her to the right. He wore a gray overcoat, open, with a navy sweater over khakis. The minute details leaped through her mind as she struggled to breath. Then he clamped a hand on her shoulder.

“Hello, Kathryn.” His voice firmed.

She couldn't help the yelp that escaped. She twisted on her heels and found herself face to face with the man she most feared. Such a benign face, until anger twisted it into the mask of a beast. The beast she'd seen strike her mother over and over until ... No, she couldn't go there. “What are you doing here?”

“I had to see you.” His eyes shimmered with tears. “You’re so much like her, you know?” He touched a piece of her hair.

She remained still, though every muscle tensed for flight.

“Do you have any idea how I’ve longed for this day? My little girl all grown up. And such a long time to find her. You changed your name. Smart move, but choosing your mother's maiden name? I'm afraid that'll cost you points.”

“I'm not playing games with you.”

“Lizzie wouldn't play either. But she was so still in the hospital bed. Helpless, really. “

She dug her nails into the palms of her hands. “How did you find her?”

“Come, come. I thought I raised you smarter than this. You may have escaped by the time you were twelve, but there are lessons you should never forget.”

“You taught me plenty of those. People are looking for you. You want to stay free? You need to get out of here.”

He moved closer. “I'll go, if you go with me.”

“I'm not a frightened kid anymore.”

“And this is Main Street.” His coat brushed against her arm. “People walking out of that store right over there. All you have to do is say one thing really loud and I'll walk away from here. Leave you be.”

“But?”

“I don't think things will work out so well for Lizzie.”

“She's your daughter.”

“Yes. I gave her life. As I gave you life. And what do you know, I can take life away.” His eyes sparked with evil. “But you already know that, don't you?”

It hurt to swallow, staring into those eyes flooded

with madness. Lizzie wouldn't stand a chance against him. Nor Jackie. JD could try to protect them, but Paul would have his way.

"I don't want to hurt you, Kathryn." His voice softened, almost childish. "I've lost so much of your life. I just want a chance to see the beautiful woman you've grown into."

"You won't harm Lizzie?"

"I wouldn't dream of it." A nasty smile twisted his face. "Well, I have, but I can let that be sufficient. If I can have you."

What choice did she have? Her folly became clear. If she'd told Marshall, he'd understand the danger. Possibly protect her. But she hadn't, being too embarrassed by her family history. She allowed her father to take her hand and draw her along the shops lining the street. Her stomach roiled at his touch and the abyss loomed.

~

They drove north nearly three hours, using back roads that wound through hills and around lakes. He turned onto a gravel road littered with weeds and stopped beneath a huge oak tree beside a dilapidated cabin. She didn't remember the broken railing, but it had been over 20 years since she'd visited as a child. The steps creaked.

"Careful. Don't want you falling through the wood and hurting yourself."

Sarcastic responses flew to her lips, but she bit them back. What good would it do to antagonize her father? Windows remained unbroken on either side of the door, though the hazy build up kept her from seeing inside. Waiting for him to open the door, leaf litter blew across her feet, rustling against the weathered boards. Paul. He didn't deserve any other distinction, but her mind kept flittering between Father and Dad. How could she think of him as anything?

The cabin seemed to breathe with the opening of the door. Its stale breath swirled across the porch, leaving a bitter smell in its wake.

"Needs a good airing." He stopped in the middle of the room and turned. Kathryn hesitated in the doorway.

"This way." Paul motioned for her to enter. Sunlight filtering through the windows revealed ancient furniture, moth battered and covered with dust. She stepped across the threshold, though her heart longed to run.

"You always were the wiser child." He gave a smile of approval.

She looked on the wall for a switch.

"No electric, don't you remember? We have the fireplace for heat. The water closets are old fashioned, but they attach to the bedrooms."

A memory tugged, but she wasn't sure she wanted to delve into it. "I've been here before?"

"Been here?" He repeated her words, outraged. "Of course, you've been here. We all have."

"I don't remember."

The simple statement threw her father into a rage. He had her by the shoulders and slammed her into the wall before she could react. His eyes teemed with anger. "We were all here. Your mother, your sister. Me. You." He slammed her again. "The four of us together."

"Enough." She pushed back. "I would have been little. You can't expect me to remember everything."

"You have to. That's why I brought you here."

"It'll come back. I just need time."

He calmed. Released her shoulders and backed away. "Of course. You have all the time you need. No one will disturb us here."

Kathryn wanted to rub her shoulders where his fingers had bit into her, but she refused to show him any sign of weakness. Paul left the cabin but returned a few moments later carrying six bags.

"You'll want to clean the cupboards first. Wouldn't want someone else getting into our groceries."

She opened her mouth for a smart retort but thought better of it. The old cast iron sink looked to be in good condition, but when she turned the faucet, nothing happened.

"You'll have to prime the pump."

Her father's voice directly behind her caused her to jump. How had he snuck that close?

She gave a blank stare and he glowered. She sighed. "Just show me."

~

Kathryn scrubbed the cabinets. The few remnants of roaches and mouse droppings didn't bother her. Her father wandering from room to room, touching surfaces, pulling objects from closets then dropping them on the floor kept her jumping. His erratic behavior had her stomach clenched. Something would strike the wide planked floor and the muscles in her neck twitched. Pain threaded through her head and shoulder. She'd refused to put on the restraining sleeve.

The corners beneath the sink became too dark to see. With a sigh of frustration, she glanced at the last place she'd seen *him*. He remained standing in the doorway of a bedroom, transfixed by something she couldn't see.

"Paul."

He gave no response.

She stood and stepped into the living room. "Paul."

Still nothing, though her voice raised. She held her hands in front of her as though she could strangle him from there. "Dad."

The word tasted like vomit, but it attracted his attention. His eyes were rimmed with red. She didn't ask why. Didn't want to know. "The sun is setting. We need candles or a lamp, so I can fix dinner."

"Dinner?" He looked at the window, seemingly surprised by the amount of time that had passed. "Can't be that late. We're going to fish for dinner."

She glanced outside. "We can go tomorrow. I'll fix spaghetti tonight."

His stance became agitated. "The plan is to fish for dinner. Get the rods from the trunk." He pulled keys from his pocket and tossed them to her.

She caught them and hesitated. He reminded her of a spoiled child about to erupt because he wouldn't be getting his way. But he wasn't a child, and eruption could prove dangerous for her. She went to retrieve the rods from the trunk of the car.

He led her along a path through some trees. More shadows than light, the wooded area lured her. Paul stopped and spun, causing her to jerk back, dropping the rods across the path.

"You know," his finger waved close to her face, "if you were to run, one daughter is as good as the other. You know that, right? It wouldn't take long for me to get Lizzie. Bring her here."

"I'm not going anywhere." Not yet. Not until she

figured out how to neutralize him. “If we’re fishing, you better hurry.” She bent to pick up the rods.

Full twilight had arrived by the time they found the pond. Crickets harmonized in the waning embers of day.

“You took too long,” he snarled at her, knocking the fishing rods from her hands.

She held up both hands. “It’s okay. I can still fix spaghetti.”

“No, you won’t. You’ll have nothing. You don’t deserve dinner.”

The idea didn’t disturb her. From his stormy glare, he thought it should. She doubted she’d be able to keep anything down. She grabbed the rods once more before he got any other ideas and stumbled back on the path they had taken.

Complete darkness had fallen when they returned to the cabin. He opened the passenger door of the car, pulled a flashlight from the glove compartment, and slammed the door closed. He stomped up the front stairs. Part of her wished he’d fall through, hurt himself bad enough to immobilize him. But no, he managed to swing the door open and light his way into the main room.

“Your room’s over here.” He stood by the second bedroom. He flashed the light through the space. She noticed a bed and a gaping hole in the wall that must be the water closet. He shoved her inside and closed the door. She heard a deadlock twist.

“Hey,” she banged on the door twice. Then left it alone. The room was completely dark, pitch black.

She hadn’t investigated the room earlier. Was the bed fresh? She doubted it. Paul had been there previously, but what had he done to make the place livable? Did she want to lay on a bed that hadn't been touched in twenty years? She sank to the floor against the door. She pressed her knees against her chest and laid her head in her lap. *Marshall, find me. Lord, show him the way.* Though she'd slept in worse conditions, the crazed man on the other side of the door made it difficult to do more than lightly doze.

Chapter 20

"Tell Kathryn to move her jeep. She can't expect to park at the impound so she's closer to the building."

"Kathryn? Is she here today?" Brenda raised her brows before searching the office area.

"Her jeep is here. She's got to be here with it. Somewhere."

"She's a good officer. You shouldn't have let her get away like that. The past few days have been downright boring."

"I'm sorry she's not here to spice things up for you. Find her and get her to move her vehicle."

He flounced to the office. Friday, and no word from her. Yes, they hadn't parted on the best of terms. And he didn't need an ungrateful wretch in his life. Allison had been like that. He shook his head. He was not thinking about Allison. He wasn't thinking about Kathryn either. Someone knocked on the door and he looked up with gratitude. "What?"

Brenda stood in the opening, looking distraught. “It is her jeep, sir. Just like you thought. But she didn't park it there. The city impounded it two days ago over on main street. The report says it sat for two days. She never moved it.”

Unease tickled his throat. “She wouldn't abandon her car. Did you call her cell?”

“No response. Went directly to voice mail.”

“Pull up tracking. See if we can locate it.” He stood, grabbed his jacket, and headed from the office.

“Where are you going?”

“Lizzie's house. Maybe it’s a misunderstanding.”

“I hope so, sir. I like her.” Brenda hurried to her desk. Marshall jogged to his vehicle. Sirens blaring, the vehicle squealed out of the parking lot.

~

“Your mother is here. I can feel her.” Paul’s voice sounded whimsical as he sauntered from room to room. Random objects were lifted from one place and returned to another.

Kathryn snuck glances at him even though she scrubbed harder to cut through the grime coating the countertops. Days ran together since he’d brought her to the cabin. Without electricity, the cabin was a haunting reminder of the past. Light shining through dingy windows revealed the squalor of each room. Each except hers. Heavy boards nailed against the window casements from the outside blocked the sun. When night fell, and he locked her into the room, darkness encased her. Like a tomb. At least he provided access to a tiny water closet.

Dust and decay brought on by years of neglect covered every surface. She cleaned what she could, but the man now lounging in the Lazy Boy cared little for the changes.

"She's here. Just as she was all those years ago." He seemed almost satisfied, a tiny smile on his face. His gaze shifted from the front door, along the east-facing wall, and up toward the ceiling. In another moment, he rested his eyes on the empty chair across the room. The chair that had belonged to Mother.

Kathryn rubbed the bruise he caused when he jerked her from it their first day at the cabin.

"You're here."

She hadn't realized his attention turned to her. She gripped the cleaning cloth.

"Your mother is here." An odd look, cunning yet barely held to sanity, glazed his eyes.

She swallowed, trying to think of distractions. "You promised to tell how you escaped after all these years." If she could turn his attention, perhaps she could stave off the plot growing in his mind.

"You would love to know, wouldn't you? Share it with all your cop friends."

"My friends have forgotten me." She stepped closer. "I really want to know. I've always known you were clever, but how did you manage to fool all of them?"

He laughed. "A fluke."

A fluke? I'm trapped in a nightmare, God, because of a fluke? She schooled her features.

"I got the wrong ID. We had similar build, similar age. I became him. He became..." He focused on her. "Dead."

"By the time the confusion cleared, you were gone."

"New staff is good for something. They were

helpful enough to search for both of you. Lizzie was the easy one to find." He pounded his fist against the arm of the chair. "Until she got herself injured while I wasn't looking." His calm facade morphed into a snarl. He shot to his feet.

Kathryn held her hands palm out, furiously thinking on how to counter his attack. "You're right. She did hurt herself and it'll take time for her to heal. You don't want to interfere with her healing, do you? Let her get better, and then we'll go see her."

"I don't want to wait." His bellow caused the windows to rattle. "Me, you, Lizzie, and Meredith. The four of us together again. That is what I want. Do you know what else I want?" He stepped closer, his tone quieting.

Kathryn refused to back away, though she held her breath.

He stopped within inches of her. "Thanksgiving dinner."

The completely unexpected response caused her to chuckle.

He grabbed the front of her shirt and slammed her against the wall. "Something wrong with Thanksgiving? With having our family together? That's what I want. And that's what I'm going to get."

Kathryn kept herself from hitting back. "Lizzie's not well. She can't leave the hospital right now."

"You would know that, wouldn't you? Being her twin and all. Always connected." He gave a shake and released her. "Do you know why I allowed your Mother to have the two of you even though it hadn't been my plan? Because there would always be an extra. If something happened to one of you, we'd have the other.

The perfect plan." He grabbed her again, this time dragging her toward the bedroom.

"She's protected. You won't be able to get near to her. If you wait..."

He paused, his face twisting in a sneer. "Oh yes, my daughter. The cop. You'd know all about protection, wouldn't you? You knew I would hate that above all else."

"I became an officer to help people. It had nothing to do with you."

"Who's going to help you? You're abandoned. Lost." He mocked, shoving her into the room. "But don't worry, I'll have Lizzie home before you know it. Behave." He pulled her closer. "Or you'll become the turkey." His threat ended with the slamming of the door and turning of the lock. A bolt also clicked into place.

She slammed her fist against the door. "Thanksgiving's not for another month," she screamed, but he didn't respond.

She stood in the dark, shaking. Anger and fear warred. He was mad, obviously, but memories of the tree branch that had become a club dripping with blood caused her breath to stick in her chest.

Chapter 21

Marshall searched the officer's report on Kathryn's jeep. No sign of a struggle. She had left it on Main Street and disappeared. He walked to the lot. He looked from the report to the windshield. The VIN numbers matched. Kathryn's jeep. No sign of a struggle. The car remained parked in the downtown area, and she disappeared. *Where are you?* The date on the initial report was three days old.

He drove to the hospital, but no unidentified bodies, living or dead, were on the records. He punched the elevator for the third floor. Turning the corner, he heard a lady laugh and a nurse exited Hayes' room. The wounded officer leaned against the bed with one hand tucked behind his head and a large grin on his face.

"Look at you." Marshal moved closer to the bed with a chuckle.

A look of guilt flashed across Hayes' face. He tried to sit taller, but Marshall pressed his shoulder not bound with bandages.

"Your stay agrees with you, don't worry about it."

Hayes shook his head. "If I don't get released soon, I may harm someone."

"That's not what I saw."

Hayes' color deepened to red. "I have to amuse myself somehow."

"What does the doctor say?"

"I'm healing."

"Good."

"But sir, I'm bored."

"What if I give you something to do? Some research?"

"Is it necessary?"

"Kathryn disappeared. They picked up her jeep on the main drag. She hasn't contacted Miami. I checked with her fellow keeping tabs on Lizzie and Jackie. Nothing. She's vanished."

"What about tracing her phone?"

Marshall shook his head. "It hasn't been replaced yet. I forgot, and then she was gone." Guilt burned his gut.

"What can I do to help?"

"Background knowledge. Something had her spooked. She wouldn't talk about it and I didn't push." Marshall shoved his hands into his pockets and looked out the window. "I should have pushed."

"Let me see what I can find. I appreciate the opportunity, sir." A different nurse entered the room and Hayes smiled. "Not even all the pretty nurses can make up for the boredom."

Marshall glanced as the woman forced a frown though her eyes sparkled, then grinned at Hayes. "She has needles. I'd be careful if I were you."

Marshall handed him the slim folder with the basics

for Kathryn and laid the laptop bag on the bed. “Machine’s fully charged. I’m sure you can get someone to plug it in when you need.” Marshall dipped his head at the nurse. She winked. “You find something the least bit interesting, give me a call. The hour doesn’t matter.” He grew serious once more. “She’s in trouble and I’d like to find her before it’s too late.”

~

Marshall squinted at the clock as he reached for the buzzing phone on the nightstand. “What did you find?”

“You said call anytime.”

“I did. What is it?”

“Brussels legally changed her name when she turned eighteen. Her real name’s Wainwright.”

“Wainwright?” Marshall searched his thoughts. “Why does that ring a bell?”

“A Paul Wainwright is on a watchlist. Escaped from Louisiana’s Penal system.”

“I don’t like coincidence.” Marshall sat up.

“I’m realizing that, sir.

“I’ll order the file for Wainwright. Good job, Hayes.”

“Thank you, sir. I should be released to rehab today. The lady nurses are starting to squabble over me.”

Marshall laughed. “Another place won’t make a difference. Maybe you should head home instead.”

“I’ll make do.”

“Check Wainwright’s records. Look into financials and real-estate.”

“Will do, sir.”

Marshall hung up. Dawn lurked a few hours away, but he was wide awake. He walked to the window and leaned against the wall. He stared into the night. Faint stars were visible. Darker shadows of houses and trees stood out along the neighborhood road.

"Where is she God?" He knew the likely scenarios but didn't want to imagine her lifeless. "Please, God." He didn't know how else to pray.

Something moved. He held his breath, uncertain what he had seen. The two-story colonial across the street remained dark. A small object bounded from the shadows. His heart calmed, only a dog. He checked the block, but nothing else moved. He padded from the window. Time for coffee.

~

Too strait-laced but keen eyes. He grinned, covering his mouth to keep his teeth from showing in the darkness. His daughter, the cop. How it made his blood boil. And she liked this one. Eventually, he'd get Lizzie. Better to aggravate the daughter he had a bit longer. Oh yes, she tried to play him. Use her skills honed over the years. But he could tell. The shadowy figure in the window disappeared. Getting rid of him would aggravate her. Oh yes, that would be fun.

Chapter 22

"The man butchered their mother. You know it's likely— "

The phone quieted, but Marshall could hear Hayes swallow. He sighed. "I know. I checked the records in Louisiana. The girls never contacted him. Officials were able to trace the facility computers. He found Lizzie using an internet ID web. Nothing for Kathryn. Finding her here may have been an unexpected bonus."

"Coincidence, sir?"

Marshall frowned. "Divine intervention? Kathryn has skills that may help her deal with him. For a while, I hope."

Hayes remained silent a moment. "At least until we find her?"

"I'm praying."

"Do you believe it makes a difference, sir?"

"Until I know what's happened to Kathryn?" He nodded. "It makes a difference to me."

"Their family home sold. Someone formed a trust

with the money, but neither of the girls touched it until ten weeks ago."

"Lizzie?"

"Yes. Eight thousand."

Marshall nodded, holding the phone to his ear. "The German tin."

"Looks that way. We'll be able to reassure Kathryn her sister isn't a criminal."

Marshall laughed. "Nothing would have convinced her otherwise. Wainwright own any other property?"

"Nothing. I sent a cruiser to check the family house, just in case, but it's been leveled, turned into a parking lot."

"He's been incarcerated twenty years. He had to take her somewhere familiar, or she'd find a way out. There has to be something. Try his parents. Or her mother's side. See what you dig up." Marshall pulled his hand through his hair. Two more days and nothing. He glowered, wondering if the glass-paneled door into the station could handle the force of his fist hitting it.

"I take a vacation and my town falls to pieces?" The familiar voice boomed through the rooms.

"Sir!" Marshall grimaced, but then relief eased his blood pressure. He grinned and shook Chief Breyer's hand. "Welcome back. You missed most of the fun." Marshall felt part of the weight slip from his shoulders.

"Fun? Five bodies at the morgue? They had to borrow a deep freeze." Breyer held his frown for a moment longer, and then burst into laughter. "Had I known the town could get this interesting, I'd have postponed my trip. Hear you did good things."

"I appreciate that, sir." Marshall followed the older man through the office doors. He took a side chair after

Breyer resumed his place behind the massive desk.

"You're still on the case."

Marshall nodded. "We believe Deputy Brussels has been kidnapped. She's out of Miami but came to town to help her sister."

"Did she find her?"

"Yes, sir. But the girl's in critical care."

"In one of these reports?" Breyer tapped the files strewn across the desk. He read from the first one he picked out of the pile. "Five men wanted for burglary in Philadelphia. All dead, but the shooter kidnapped the cop?"

"Unrelated." He wrinkled his forehead. "Sort of. It's her father. He escaped from the state pen in Louisiana. He was serving life without parole for murdering his wife."

"She isn't helping her dad?"

"Not possible. Reports say the girls witnessed the attack. It was brutal, then he took them to dinner at Denny's. Manager called the police because they were splattered with blood."

Breyer curled his lip. "Foul matters. My Escalade got juice? Thought I'd drop in on Officer Hayes. Give him an earful for getting shot."

"I'd have spit-shined her, sir, had I known you'd be here today."

He laughed. "You're a good man, Franklin."

"Probably something to do with you."

They shook hands once more. Breyer glanced at the Captain's chair. "How did you like the feel?"

Marshall grinned. "More comfortable than expected, sir."

"I'll be retiring one of these days. It would be an

honor to recommend you for the position."

"Not too soon."

"Back to work, son." He slapped Marshall on the shoulder and exited the office.

Marshall returned to the captain's chair and powered on the monitor. As his finger touched the s-key, an explosion rattled the windows and shook the floor.

~

Kathryn rubbed the worn towel against the porcelain plate and reached for another dish stacked beside the sink.

"I'm in the mood for a ride, what do you say?" Paul glanced at her.

She stopped drying. "Where are we going?" Over a week and she hadn't stepped foot outside. Why today? What did he want to show her? What was he up to?

"Out someplace." He sounded noncommittal, like it didn't matter. But his sly glance sent shivers across her skin. "I'm in the mood to watch TV."

She refused to allow him access to her fear. Instead, she hung the towel on the metal ring attached to the cabinet and placed the plate on the counter. By the time she turned around, he stood near the door putting his arms through his corduroy jacket. He jangled keys. "If I allow you to come with me, you have to behave."

He tried to hide it, but she could tell he wanted her to go. Would even force her if she made an issue of it.

"If you behave." He repeated, taking four steps toward her. He stood a breath away.

She forced herself to look up and meet his eyes. Laughter lurked in their depth. A secret amused him greatly. Her stomach dropped but she forced a grin.

"I promise I'll be Daddy's perfect little girl." The words left a bitter taste in her mouth, but hope lightened her heart. *One mistake, one distraction, and we can end this nightmare.* She sent her gaze heavenward then followed her father to the front door.

"Grab your sweater."

Twenty years of disuse hadn't spoiled the Oldsmobile. She buckled herself into the front seat. Her heart dipped. The handle and lock mechanism had been removed from the passenger seat door.

"Child safety precaution. You know how careful I've always been."

"You were." She kept her voice light. "You did some good things as a dad."

"Like what? Tell me." He started the car and pulled away from the cabin.

Memories of screams and blood tried to blot everything from her thoughts, but she forced herself into the earlier years.

"The beach in New Jersey. Where was it?" She looked at him.

He smiled. "Ocean City."

~

"Captain Breyer is dead." Marshall felt numb saying the words to Hayes. "The black SUV blew up." *It should have been him.*

"I heard. This can wait."

"What did you find?"

"A cabin. Kathryn's grandmother Malinda Brussel owned it. The trust kept it in her name, over in Lake County."

"Email the address."

"Gotcha, boss." Silence, and then Hayes cleared his

throat. “Oh man, I’m sorry.”

“We all are. We’re going to get him. For Breyer. For Kathryn. For everyone. Louisiana can have the pieces.”

He pressed end and dialed the extension for the front desk.

“Yes, Sergeant Franklin?” Brenda’s voice wobbled with tears.

“Contact Dennis. Have them do a sweep of the Buick. I want it at the door in five.”

“Yes, sir.”

Chapter 23

"Hey there." Marshall lifted his mirrored sunglasses to the top of his head. "I'm lookin' for the Brussel cabin. Got word it'll be on the market in a few months. Thought I'd take a sneak peek."

"That old place?" The old man spit into a cup. "Nothin' good there."

"There's land. Developers gonna try to snap it up. My grandmother's place out by Riley's Lake …" He shook his head, frowning. "No decent folk can get close to it. I'd hate to see it happen here."

"What would you do?" Wizened eyes surveyed him.

Marshall grinned. "Fish."

The old man relaxed slightly. "I doubt a city slicker like yourself would know anything 'bout fishin'."

"Might surprise you with a good angus fly on my line."

Minutes later Marshall returned the glasses to his face and tightened his grip on the map. He drove the paved road until he saw the elm that had been split by lightning. The dead half pointed to the road he wanted to take. He pulled off.

The unpaved path showed recent tracks, several from the same vehicle going back and forth. A different set of tracks could be noticed. He continued a little further on the paved road until he found a place to hide the Buick. Its navy-blue color blended into the pines, elm, and oak forest surrounding him. He grabbed the black pack, holstered his weapon, and strapped a .38 special to the back of his belt.

He jogged his way to the trail he wanted.

Finding the cabin proved relatively easy. Deeper ruts in the dirt marked where a car normally parked. The building was dark. It should have a disused aura in the early afternoon light, but the porch had been swept clean. He crept along the perimeter. No power. No generator. No signs of life. He didn't want to risk stepping onto the front porch. Two windows had been boarded. The next two had wooden dowels placed so the window couldn't be lifted. Peering through a side window, he saw a kitchen table and chairs. He slipped his knife between the lock and the window. The old lock slid open. He listened. Only the wind rustled the leaves and trees creaked. He pushed the window up. He dropped his bag inside first. Nothing happened. With a prayer of protection on his lips, he pulled himself over the windowsill and into the cabin.

No one was home, but dishes sat on a cloth by the sink. He could hope. Oh, he could hope. He pulled the backpack on, closed and locked the window, and checked the area. No sign of his entry. He began to search.

He swept his flashlight across the pitch-black

bedroom with boarded windows. Partway through the search, rumblings of a car could be heard. Dowsing the light, he found a corner away from the door, using a dresser to block him from sight if need be. He waited.

A car door slammed. Someone screamed gibberish or a foreign language, he couldn't tell. But upset. Angry. The voice bellowed, then turned into a high-pitched whine. It drew closer. There were words in the nonsense, but the second voice grabbed his attention. He drew his weapon, using the furious ranting to hide the sound of sliding a bullet into the chamber.

Kathryn. She reasoned with the madman, although her voice sounded stressed. Pained. Then she burst into the room. He heard her stumble. The door slammed shut and two locks engaged. She pounded her fist against the door, shouting, and then went silent. He could hear her breathing. She remained at the door. He heard something tap, as though she laid her head against the door. The ranting outside continued, though it grew softer. Wainwright moved away from them.

Marshall stepped from his hiding place. Stealth, step by step, he moved closer to where she should be. He didn't dare turn on the flashlight. Something crashed elsewhere in the house.

"Kathryn," he whispered then grabbed her when he felt her move. Covered her mouth with his hand. Her elbow cracked into his side and he gasped. Then she turned and flung her arms around his neck.

~

"You scared me half to death." She whispered, still holding him tight. *How had he found her?*

"And you cracked my rib." Then he did what she'd longed for. He kissed her. Not a gentle kiss, this one could start a fire. She kissed him back. Because he made her feel alive.

The cocking of a twelve gauge drew them apart. Wainwright blasted one of the cabin walls.

Marshall turned toward the door. "What is he— "

She pushed him away, in the direction of the water closet. She guided him through the darkness. They both paused when they heard shells drop on the ground outside the locked room.

"Kathryn…" His hand felt good against her cheek, but she couldn't linger. She had to keep Dad from noticing him.

"Stay put."

"No way." He pushed against her.

"He wants to scare me." She kept her voice soft. "You were supposed to be in the SUV." She reached out and felt his chest. His heart still beat. "He intended the bomb to kill you."

"Breyer returned early. It was his SUV."

She heard him swallow, felt his body shudder.

His breath tickled her ear. "I have a weapon."

"Then use it if you have a shot. But he won't kill me, not yet. He wants my sister and me together. The three of us. Then I don't know what will happen."

The shotgun charged again.

"Let's end this before we have to find out." He kissed her again, but she pulled away, raced to the middle of the room. The first lock clicked open. There wasn't time to say the three words that clung to her heart. *I love you.* She whispered them anyway. Another lock turned. She wrapped her arms around her middle and schooled her features to show no hope. *Help us God.* She prayed. The door swung on its hinges until it hit the wall.

~

Light from the other room put her father in silhouette, but she could see the gun pointed at her chest. “What are you doing?”

He took a step into the room. “I wanted to kill something today.” He pouted like a child bereft of a favored toy.

“You did. Someone was in that car.”

The madman’s voice reverberated. “It wasn’t *him.* He thought he was clever. You thought he was clever.” He shoved the shotgun closer. “That SUV stayed at his house. Greed is a sin. He deserved to die.” He took another step into the room.

Kathryn backed up a step. If he got past the door, Marshall would have a clean shot.

He snarled at her. “I shouldn’t care, should I? Maybe, if I kill you, I won’t care anymore.”

Kathryn threw her hands up. “Make up your mind. You want Lizzie, then you don’t. You want a special dinner, then you don’t. You want to kill me, then you don’t. How am I supposed to keep up?” She didn’t need to fake the tears choking her voice.

His loud voice softened to a whine. “Can’t a man change his mind?”

She sobbed as the weapon drifted down until the barrel faced the floor.

“I’ll get her. I will, you’ll see this time.” He tapped the barrel on the floor. “We’ll be together. The three of us, here, with your mother. I feel her haunting this place.” He backed away and pulled the door shut.

Kathryn nearly fell to her knees. Locks clicked into place again. Marshall caught her.

The rumble of the Oldsmobile came through the walls, getting softer until silence returned. Marshall pressed the flashlight button and light spilled across the knotted pine floor.

"You brought a light."

She looked about ready to cry, her eyes large, bruised by fatigue and fear.

"Don't go all soft on me now. I won't know how to handle it."

She slapped his arm. Hard. "Let's get out of here."

"Yes, ma'am." He made a show of rubbing his arm. The sound of her giggle pleased him. "Which way?"

"I would love to shoot the hinges from the door, but the longer we get before he realizes we're gone …" She tilted her head at the boarded windows. "What do you think?"

He swung his pack around and placed it on the floor. "Good thing I brought a crowbar."

"I'm going to kiss you when we get out of here."

"Why wait?" He grabbed her. The connection between his lips and hers made her heart beat faster. Infused her with light.

She moaned, pulling away. "Good as this is, we don't have time. He could be hours or twenty minutes."

"Let's scram."

By wedging the bar between the window opening and the board, they were able to push the nails from the side of the house. Within an hour, dim light poured through the open window. A cool breeze caused him to shiver. Kathryn felt it too, rubbing her bare arms. He glanced around the room. "Got warmer clothes?"

She ran to a closet and pulled a heavy sweater over her T-Shirt. She tied another around her waist. "Just in case."

"Ladies first." He offered his hand. She squeezed, and then dove through the window, rolling across the ground and jumping to her feet. "Show off."

The sound of an engine revving stopped them in their tracks. Marshall turned toward the front of the cabin where the driveway ended. Kathryn felt her heart trip and her body went cold.

"Dad." She grabbed Marshall's arm and ran into the line of trees. A cold mist blew through the air as they entered the woods.

"Just what we need."

She heard Marshall mutter. She pushed him on. "Think of it as a blessing in disguise. If it rains, our tracks will wash away."

He grunted.

They kept moving, across a trail and into the brush. Her extra sweater tangled in the thorns. She jerked it free.

"How well do you know these woods?" Marshall asked, helping pull her away from the brambles. They faced a thick tree trunk fallen across the ground, and he offered his hand.

"Not well." She used him for leverage and jumped. "Dad brought us. We weren't encouraged to explore."

"The place belongs to your mother. Did you know that?"

"Mom?" She glanced in his direction. "Dad always acted like it was his." They crossed another rough patch of earth and she grabbed his hand. She took a deep breath. "I'm sorry I didn't tell you about him sooner. If I had trusted— "

"I understand." He squeezed her hand. "I didn't like

it at the time, but I wouldn't have believed the extent of his sickness without witnessing it myself. You're an amazing woman, Punk."

"Sure." She drenched her voice with sarcasm. "Now you tell me." The warmth of his voice chased chills from her arms. "We're in a strange wood being chased by a madman, and I have no weapon."

"You're not a certified black belt?"

"Ha. I'd prefer something usable from a distance."

Marshall stopped, and she bounced into him.

He laughed. "Must have forgotten my blinker." He turned and pulled the .38 from beneath his jacket. "My first gift for you." He held it for her to take.

"Wow." The tiny gun felt better than it looked. "Real bullets in this thing or blanks?"

His smile teased her into smiling herself.

"Thank you." She shook her head and gave him a shove. "Let's move." She tucked it into her pocket. Definitely felt better.

Marshall slapped his forehead. "The old man gave me a map." He proceeded to pull paper from the front pocket of the backpack.

Kathryn rubbed her arms and bounced on her feet. "We really need to move. Moving will make me warmer."

"You've been in Miami too long." He looked from the map to their surroundings, and back at the map. "We need to find the road."

"It's too risky going back for the car. Dad may have found it. Could be why he returned so quickly." She still shivered, even though Marshall resumed moving forward. The mist turned to rain.

Marshall lifted his face to the sky. She could see

water streaming down his cheeks.

"Me being from Miami, I prefer my weather a tad warmer." Cold set in as she got soaked to the skin. "What made you become a cop?" She shivered, pulling herself through another bramble bush.

He wrapped an arm around her shoulder, but not much warmth seeped into her. She felt cold lips touch near her eye. The connection was better than walking alone.

His voice vibrated through her. "My family. My Dad, an uncle, couple of cousins—all either police or fire. Could say it's in our blood. God made the Franklin men to be protectors. Women too." He reassured her after a moment's pause. "Lacey's in social work."

"Does she live nearby?"

He held a thick branch so they could crawl under it. "She's in Chicago."

"Have you been to Chicago?"

"Allison and I visited her."

"Who?" Why did another woman's name on his lips irritate her?

"My fiancé. Ex-fiancé."

"What happened?"

"Didn't work out."

"Stupid, huh?"

"What? I made mistakes, but I wouldn't say I was stupid."

"Not you. Her. Any woman that let you go would have to be stupid."

"Think so, huh?"

She could hear the smile dripping through his tone. Then a different sound drowned away their companionable banter.

They stopped. "Moped?" Marshall asked in a quiet voice.

She shrugged her shoulders. "We have to assume it's him."

"We're still miles from the road. We need to find thicker bushes or a shelter. Rain's making the trail slippery."

"Too good to last." Kathryn pushed herself into a jog. Marshall matched her steps. He tugged her sleeve and pointed at a bush-filled crevice.

They crawled beneath the branches and hunkered in the middle of the patch. She couldn't see much, but the struggling motor of an old bike grew louder. He curled his body over hers, and they both peeked through the crisscross of plants. Her toes began to shiver. Time slowed. the sound grew louder. She held her breath. The engine hiccupped across uneven ground, and then the noise faded into a different direction. They remained hidden, Marshall's arms wrapped around her, until silence reigned once more.

She touched his cheek. Her cold fingers could feel stubble on his face. He wrapped her hand in both of his and breathed warmth onto it. With a wobbly smile, she crawled on her belly to get out of the ditch. He joined her, and they continued. The light splatter of rain soaked her to her skin, but her heart held a spark of warmth.

The hairs on her arms shivered, possibly even her eyelids. Kathryn placed one foot in front of the other, doggedly following Marshall. Though the drizzle of rain has ceased, cold air embraced them. He paused, and she bumped into his back once more. Her senses alerted, but no immediate danger surfaced. He pulled a bottle of water from his pack and handed it to her.

"No coffee?" She teased through chattering teeth.

"How about chocolate?" he held a bar in his hand.

She grabbed it. "You are a good man, Sarge."

Not far off, a truck rumbled on a road, its sound escalating and then descending as it continued its way.

"We're close." Marshall adjusted the map.

Relief helped her smile. She drank another swig of water and dropped the bottle into the pack. She kept the chocolate, popping another three sections into her mouth. The sweet cocoa flavor almost helped her forget the bone-chilling forest. They followed the sound of the truck.

Twenty minutes later, Kathryn crouched beside a tall pine. A shoulder of grass separated her from the road. "Nothing." She checked both directions again.

Marshall knelt beside her, resting his hand on her shoulder. She looked at him. The afternoon sun crept through the clouds, creating a yellow haze around them. Weary, cold, and determined—she could see it in his face. "If we head that way," he nodded to the south, "we'll pass through Wesher."

Kathryn sighed. "Can we get there before dark?"

He wrapped his hand against her head and pulled the two of them together. It wasn't a kiss, but his touch brightened her spirit. "We'll follow the road. If we hear something, duck into the woods."

She hugged him back.

Chapter 24

"I've been waiting patiently all afternoon. I'd rather not shoot you in the back." Paul held a gun steady, his cold eyes daring Marshall to try and run. Marshall could feel Kathryn droop behind him. Every ounce of effort to get themselves to safety, and he'd led them into a trap.

Paul wiggled his weapon. "Get your gun out nice and easy and place it on the counter."

Marshall complied, glancing at Kathryn. Her face looked hard and her eyes watchful. She wasn't ready to give in. He offered a tiny smile of encouragement before facing Paul.

"Get the weapon you gave my daughter. Or you end up like the shopkeeper. A man his age ought to know how to listen."

Kathryn pulled the tiny gun from her pocket. "Deadly force? Is that your answer to everything?" Her voice tinged with anger. She stepped beside Marshall to scowl at her father.

"It's worked in the past. Why change?"

"Worked?"

Marshall reached for the .38.

She saw him, and stepped in front, partially blocking him from view. "You spent twenty years in maximum security. How did that work for you? Lizzie and I spent our teen years with your batty older sister. That worked?"

Paul's face reddened. "You always were self-centered. I did what needed to be done. To your mother. To you. You all deserved it."

Marshall fired the .38 at the hand holding the shotgun. With a scream of pain, Paul dropped the weapon. He tossed the special to Kathryn and kicked the shotgun from Paul's feet. He picked up his weapon from the counter and aimed it at the older man.

Paul cupped his good hand around the wounded one. Blood dripped on the floor. The cold blue eyes focused behind him. He turned. Kathryn's hand shook as she faced her father. He could feel her struggle. "He's unarmed, Punk."

"I see that." The weapon steadied. "He deserves to die for all the lives he's destroyed."

"It won't fix any of those lives. You can't bring them back. All you can do is offer mercy."

Her lip curled. "I'm not feeling mercy." She lowered the gun.

"That's right, honey. Give me another chance. Next time will be perfect." Paul grinned at her.

"Shut up." She growled and turned away.

Marshall kept his attention fixed on Paul. "Call the station, Punk. I'll feel better when this man is delivered to the cell where he belongs."

"Yes, dear. Pick up the phone. Make that call. Time to be a good cop."

The look of gleeful madness on Paul's face caused Marshall's stomach to drop. "Hold off on that call." He shouted.

"Yeah, I got that." Kathryn sounded right behind him.

Paul swayed on his feet and allowed blood to drip on the top of his tennis shoes. "Long afternoons bore me." He looked at the door, at the top of the door.

Marshall noticed a slim black wire across the door frame. The store had been rigged to explode.

~

Kathryn found a devise connected to the phone. Anger surged. She squelched the emotion. Marshall's arm wrapped around her and she stiffened.

"There is more than one devise." He whispered. She nodded and focused on Dad. "The front door is rigged."

"Phone, too. He's been in the back as well."

"How do you know?"

"Blood by the register, but no body. He moved it."

"Doesn't he realize any kind of blast is likely to kill him, too?"

Kathryn watched Paul lift a towel and wrap his hand. He pulled a straight-backed wood chair away from the checkers table set up in the front window and sat down. He looked suspiciously calm.

"Watch him. I'm going to check the back."

"Punk," Marshall shook his head, but she refused to listen. Dying here wasn't an option. She wanted something better.

She checked the swinging door leading into a different room. No wires. She gave a gentle push, and it opened slightly before swinging toward her. The room behind had light, and she glimpsed someone laid out on the floor. She pushed a little harder and slipped into the room.

A large freezer took up one side of the room. Shelves packed with boxes filled another. In front of the shelves lay an older man.

~

Paul settled into the hard chair and crossed his right leg over the left. "You aren't good enough for her."

Marshall split his attention between Paul and finding the devise connected to the wire. The older man rested casually. He could have been at a dinner party. The lead wires disappeared into a cereal box.

"Where did you learn to set explosives?"

Paul shrugged. "Roommates come in handy sometimes."

"Why this place?" He didn't dare move the box without knowing more. He crossed the store. "If the bomb goes off, you're dead like the rest of us."

Paul's eyes gleamed. "It doesn't have to go off."

"What do you want?"

Paul raised his good hand, studied the nails, and then rubbed them against his shirt. He tilted his head to look at Marshall. "I want Kathryn to leave with me."

"That's not going to happen."

His face tightened. "Then we all die."

Marshall checked his phone again. No service. How could he get help?

"I'll go."

He swung around. Kathryn stood by the counter.

"No."

She pointed to the swinging door. "The man back

there needs help now. There isn't time to argue."

"Even if you go, you know he won't keep his word."

She faced her father. "He leaves first. With the old man."

Paul didn't look pleased, and Marshall agreed with him for once. "I'm not leaving you with him."

She stepped around him, far enough away that he couldn't grab her. "Today you are."

"I really am surprised he hasn't died yet." Paul rose from the chair. "Get the shopkeeper and go to the front door."

Marshall gripped the handle of the Glock. "Punk, this is not a good idea."

"It's the only one I have, Sarge."

Paul grinned. "I'd hurry. Shopkeeper dies and the deals off."

~

Marshall struggled within himself as he slipped through the swinging door. Oh man. he rubbed his face, exhaustion and failure threatening to overwhelm him. The old man who'd provided the map lay on the concrete in a blood-soaked shirt. He pressed against the shopkeeper's neck. A thread pulse pushed beneath his fingers. He tucked his gun in its holster and lifted the old man. The weathered face rolled to the side, his mouth gaping open. He backed through the door and reentered the store. They were gone.

Kathryn.

He ran to the door, the burden in his arms dragging him. He checked the lot, but no sign of them. Then he heard a car starting behind the building. They were getting away.

He checked the door. A wire hung loose, but he had no faith in Paul.

"What do I do, God?"

The old man drew a shaky breath. They needed out now. A sign lit in the center of the picture window.

Idiot.

He laid the old man on the ground and picked up the hard chair where Paul had sat. He closed his eyes. *God, please*. He swung the chair with all his might at the glass window. Sparks flew when the lit sign popped. Glass shattered, jagged pieces dropping from the top of the window to the floor.

He started to lift the old man, but then felt for a set of keys. He fished them from a front pocket. He stepped over the sharp peaks of glass sticking up from the bottom of the window. The front lot remained empty. He ran around the side of the building. A classic yellow Ford truck had been parked beneath the streetlamp. "I hope it drives better than it looks."

He jogged. As he reached the passenger door, a bright light flared from behind. An instant later, percussion knocked him against the metal door. A ball of fire plumed into the night sky. Debris rained down.

Ears ringing, he flung the door open and set his burden in the seat. He could feel heat from the fire as he ran to the driver's side. The truck started beautifully, and he roared out of Wesher.

Within three minutes he had bars on his phone.

Chapter 25

"It's over, Wainwright."

The look of surprise on Paul's face made Marshall want to laugh. The fifth-floor hospital room with white walls and beeping machines didn't hold Lizzie. The mad rush from Wesher to Tampa General had paid off.

Paul backed up, but another officer blocked the doorway. In a matter of seconds, the older man stood with his face pressed against the wall and Marshall clipped the handcuffs.

"My hand." Paul shouted and tried to pull away. Marshall twisted him around.

"Your hand gets medical attention when I get Kathryn."

Paul snarled. "You won't find her."

Marshall grabbed him by the lapels of his jacket and slammed him against the wall. "I know how long it took you to get here and where you were coming from. I'll find her."

"We'll take him, Sergeant."

Marshall wanted to pound until he received answers, but the pair of agents standing in the door didn't approve. They pulled Paul's arm and tugged him out of reach.

"Wait." Marshall hooked Paul's pocket. "I want his keys."

Paul tried to twist around, but an agent grabbed him by the scruff of his neck, holding him immobile. Marshall smirked. He fished keys from the front jeans pocket. "Get him back where he belongs, and make sure they don't lose him again."

Adrenaline pumped his body. He didn't wait for an elevator but ran down the stairs and sprinted across the main floor lobby into the parking area. He heard other officers following.

"You have the bolo for the car." He shouted without turning around. "Spread out and find it." He raced down the center aisle.

"Over here."

He looked up and saw someone waving a beam of light in a dark area of the lot. He ran.

The car belonged to Wainwright, but they already had the empty front and back seats lit up. "She's not here, sir," someone said.

She had to be. "Trunk." He directed.

He used the key, ignored the screech of the hinges, and tapped the large tarp filling the space. Something moved beneath it. He threw it aside.

Kathryn. Marshall brushed aside her hair and pressed his fingers against her neck. He could feel her pulse. "Thank you, God." He bowed his head with a sigh of relief.

"We need a gurney?" An attendant asked.

Marshall shook his head. "I've got her." He moved the tarp and lifted her in his arms. Her head fell back. Her arms and feet were taped. He shrugged his arm so her head lolled against his shoulder. "This is not a habit I like, Punk." He carried her to the emergency entrance.

In a matter of minutes, he paced the front hallway while the evening crew worked on Kathryn.

"Hope they can afford to replace their tiles." JD teased.

Marshall crossed his arms. Not the man he wanted to see.

"How is she?"

Marshall shrugged. "They kicked me out."

"What happened?"

"He must have hit her and knocked her out. How many times can a person be hit in the head and something bad not happen?"

JD grinned. "She's pretty hard-headed."

"You got that right. How's Lizzie?"

"Awake. Well, wakeful. She looks around. Falls asleep. Seems to enjoy listening to Jackie read to her."

"Jackie's not staying in the hotel?"

"Did you really expect that woman to stay put? Besides, it helps her stay focused. I found her wandering around looking for Hayward the first night."

A doctor entered the area and Marshall crossed the room. "I'm Sergeant Franklin. How's my officer?"

"We don't have a police officer in the back." The balding doctor frowned.

"The woman you were working on. You kicked me out of the room."

"Oh, I didn't realize. She's got a nasty headache. There's also bruising around her cheek and eye. Older, but it's there. Someone hitting her?"

"We arrested him. She's awake? She'll be okay?"

"I'd like to keep her overnight. Observation for a concussion. She's not happy."

JD shook his head. "She won't stay."

"Let me talk to her," Marshall shoved his hands in his pockets. "If she stays, she'll be able to see Lizzie in the morning."

JD motioned with his hand. "Give it a try."

Marshall followed the doctor. JD's view of Kathryn differed from his own. She sat on the edge of the hospital bed, wincing at a tender spot behind her right ear. "If it hurts, you should leave it alone."

"Thanks, doc." She grimaced at Marshall. "Are we ready to get out of here?" She made to stand, but he pressed against her shoulder, keeping her on the bed.

"Let me guess. They offered you pain meds and you've left them in the plastic cup on the counter. They told you to spend the night for observation because of the concussion, but you've refused."

She glared at the doctor. "He didn't say it was absolutely mandatory."

"Well," Marshall leaned closer. "Unless you want to walk to your sister's house, we'll be staying here."

"How far is it?"

"We're in Tampa."

"What? How'd we get here?"

"Your father came for Lizzie. We surprised him."

A shadow caused her eyes to darken. "The gas station exploded."

"Here, sit back. At least hold the ice pack on your head." He adjusted the bed so she could sit up. "The old man had an amazing classic Ford truck. We were on our way before the station blew."

She gasped at the cold compress but leaned back. "What am I doing here?"

"I took the old man to the nearest hospital. There weren't too many choices for Wainwright. He couldn't risk returning to the cabin. I took a chance he'd come here for your sister."

"Lizzie's safe?"

He nodded. "I called JD, warned him to get her moved. We set up in the room. Paul showed up, and we got him with almost no fuss. FBI took him. He'll be processed and returned to Louisiana."

"It's over." She closed her eyes for a moment, then tried to push herself up. "What about Lizzie? I have to see her."

"She's resting. We'll visit her in the morning. JD says she's in and out of consciousness."

"Where's Jackie?"

"At the hotel. I'll head back there and get you first thing in the morning."

"How about you stay in the hospital and I go back to the hotel?"

He put his hand on the bed and leaned closer. "You need to stay here one night and not get into any trouble. Think you can manage that?"

A woman's voice disturbed them. "Is this man bothering you?"

"Yes," Kathryn laughed. "He won't let me leave."

Marshall stood, holding his hands up against the nurse's glare. "She's trying to circumvent doctor orders."

The nurse checked her paperwork, took Kathryn's arm and scanned the bar code. She checked the reading.

"Kathryn Brussels?"

"Yes."

"They'll move you to the second floor. You're only here for observation, so you don't need a port."

"What's a port?"

"For an IV."

"I don't know. Maybe if you hook her up, she won't try to escape." Marshall grinned at Kathryn.

The nurse didn't seem amused. Her frown deepened. "Visiting hours are over."

"I'm a police officer." Marshall showed the nurse his badge. "I'm not leaving until I see her settled in a room."

"I'm sorry, I didn't realize." She pointed at the two of them. "Still, if you upset her, officer or not, you're out of here." The woman departed, no improvement to her scowl.

Kathryn lifted a brow. "Hear that? You're out 'a here."

"I should tell JD what's going on, but I'm not leaving."

"Is he down here? He's supposed to be watching over Lizzie. Why's he here?"

"He came down for a moment to see what happened. Your sister's fine. You'll see her in the morning. Lord willing, she'll be awake and able to tell us a few things."

"Marshall …"

He knew memories of today, the past few days, surfaced when her cheeks paled, and her lips pulled down. He grabbed her hand. "Right now, you need to rest. Take the pain killers."

"You lost your chief."

“The entire county lost.” The weight of grief nearly overwhelmed him for a moment. The feel of Kathryn’s hand wrapping around his kept him together. He pushed back tears and the thick knot in his throat. “Let me talk to JD.”

Had it really happened in just one day? His mind whirled on his return to the waiting area. The explosion, a solid lead on Kathryn and her father, their desperate race for help only to end up pawns in a madman’s lair. Weariness washed through him.

He found JD, and then located Kathryn in her observation room. He didn’t have the energy to walk to the hotel. In the end, he pulled a chair close to the bed and propped his feet up. He fell asleep listening to the bustle of the hospital ward.

Chapter 26

"What are you doing here?"

Marshall jumped at Kathryn's voice. He rubbed his face. "What time is it? Are you okay?" He glanced at the window. The first touches of morning caused the sky to glow. "How's your head?"

She groaned. "Attached and not letting me forget it." She swung her legs over the edge of the bed.

"Let me help." He reached his arm toward her, then tugged when she wrapped her hand around his. "Steady?" He waited for her nod before releasing her.

"I'm going to use the little girl's room, and then you can take me to Lizzie."

The fact she declared instead of asked made him grin. "Yes, ma'am."

He stretched, then rubbed the itchy shadow growing across his cheeks and chin. A toothbrush and razor would not go amiss.

Kathryn returned with her hair combed and the scent of mint on her breath.

"Got an extra toothbrush in there?"

She shrugged. "Wash and use the one that's there."

He couldn't do anything about shaving, but clean teeth was a good start. Kathryn stood at the door when he returned. "Ready?" She asked, stepping into the hall.

He motioned to the elevators. "Fourth floor."

~

Lizzie slept. Kathryn felt tension ease from her shoulders. The litany of machines reduced to a monitor and an IV bag. Even better, Paul's ugliness didn't encroach on Lizzie. The orange-colored dawn cast a glow through the room. Someone had brushed her hair. Her sleep seemed natural.

"Much better than the last time we saw her," Marshall spoke in hushed tones.

Kathryn backed into him. "I don't want to wake her."

They walked further down the hall. "Was it worth spending the night in the hospital?"

She grinned at Marshall. "This once. Yes, I'm glad we stayed."

"I have to get back home. Do you want to stay with Jackie and JD?"

Staying would be easy, but Marshall would have to face the mess of the past few days on his own. She shook her head. "I'm going with you."

"Not to work. You're still battling a concussion. I'll take you home."

Kathryn rolled her eyes, but weariness kept her from protesting.

~

He'd dropped Kathryn at the house then spent hours staring at files and screens without really seeing. To stay was useless, even though it was only mid-afternoon. "I'm going home. Call my cell if there's a problem." Marshall told the temp at the large desk in the main room.

He hesitated before opening the door to his Buick. The far side of the parking lot still smelled of rancid smoke. Wainwright would be charged, but what could you add to the life sentence of a madman? The car was quiet. He didn't bother turning on the radio. Go home? He turned in the wrong direction. Check on Kathryn first. He used the hidden key to let himself in. The house was quiet.

Marshall walked through the kitchen. He'd been furious with her. Now, he wanted to hold her and let her know a father like Paul Wainwright wouldn't frighten him away. He pulled a small silver pan onto the stove and gathered cocoa ingredients. Kathryn hadn't appeared by the time the drink was ready. He fixed himself a cup, covered the pot and turned the burner off, then went and sat on the couch. The hot chocolate tasted smooth but enhanced his weariness. Maybe he could rest for a few minutes. He stretched out on the couch.

~

It was early evening when Kathryn padded into Lizzie's living room in bare feet. The light above the stove lit the kitchen, but the living room remained shadowed. She could just make out the shape of someone buried beneath a blanket on the couch. It better be Marshall. She inched closer and noticed the scruffy hair. She smiled, heading to the kitchen,

A saucepan had been pushed to the back burner. She lifted the lid and a wave of chocolate plumed into the air. She inhaled deeply. She turned the burner to low and then pulled a mug from the open shelf beside the stove. The couch squeaked, and she brought down a second cup.

"I already have a cup. figured you'd need sleep more than cocoa." Marshall stopped at the kitchen doorway.

She stirred the milky mixture. "You thought wrong."

"You look like you feel better."

She couldn't disagree. "Much. Sleeping in my own bed helped."

"Your sister's place starting to feel like home? You like our little corner of the world?"

She scoffed. "I had fewer problems in Miami." She took his mug. "Sit at the table and I'll bring you a mug."

He stepped closer to protest. "I should get it."

"I'm fine. I've got this, go have a seat."

"Ma'am, yes ma'am."

She managed to get most of the mixture into the mugs. She dug an open package of marshmallows and plopped five into hers.

"Make mine a handful." Marshall called from the table.

"I have small hands."

"No, you don't. I've seen that gun you handle."

She shook her head. She gave him one. It looked lonely. When she brought the cups to the table, floating white blobs covered his.

"Perfect."

"We'll see how it tastes." She sat at the end of the table. She picked up a photo of Lizzie and her. "I hope Lizzie can get home soon."

He interrupted her darkening thoughts. "Hey. Drink

your chocolate. Save the other thoughts for tomorrow."

"What do I think about tonight?"

He leaned forward. "You are sitting across from a super hunk of a man, and your life hasn't been threatened in…" He looked at his watch. "Eighteen hours."

"He may be hunky, and he may be right. But that doesn't give me a whole lot to think about."

He grabbed his chest. "I'm wounded."

She drank, slightly amused. Warm chocolate dipped in milk flowed across her tongue, soothed the ache in her throat. She closed her eyes and enjoyed more.

"You do like your cocoa." Marshall teased her.

She gave him a satisfied smile. "The cook prepared it perfectly."

"You have marshmallow on your lip."

"I what?" She couldn't finish because he stretched across the small table and kissed her. He licked the gooey sweet from her lips, and then kissed her properly. The way a woman in love wanted to be kissed. She gave in for a moment then pushed him away. A woman in love? Where had that thought come from?

"I don't think I've ever liked hot chocolate as much as I do now."

Heat infused her face, and she brought the mug to her lips. She heard him laughing softly. "Fun as this is, I think I need more sleep."

"I'll be here. Make sure everything's in order."

"You can't stay in the house while I sleep."

"I'm here. Doctor's orders."

"Yeah. Not my doctor. He looked ready to shoot you." She giggled.

He picked up both mugs from the table. "Bed. I'll

clean up the mess."

She saluted him this time. "Yes, Sarge."

He placed the cups on the counter and caught her in his arms.

The heat of a moment ago had cooled. She rested her head on his chest and wrapped her arms around his waist.

He kissed the top of her head. "Sweet dreams, Punk."

Chapter 27

Marshall sat behind the massive desk of Breyer's office in the still of the morning. No, his office now. The weight on his shoulders caused his neck to cramp. Breyer was dead. The man responsible on his way back to prison. Perhaps a needle in the arm would bring a well-deserved death, but it wouldn't resurrect Breyer.

"Hey, boss." Brenda leaned against the door jamb. She held a large white envelope. "This came yesterday from the forensic team in Orlando."

"Orlando?" He strode to get the package. "They found something on Jackie's computer stuff?"

"Aren't they all dead, though?"

"Kathryn's dad wrapped 'em up with a tidy bow." He tossed the envelope on the desk. "Thanks." There were reports to be typed. He returned to his seat, leaned over and pulled his laptop from its bag. "Welcome to the twenty-first century," he informed the desk.

An hour into typing reports, Marshall leaned back,

rubbing his hands over his eyes. Based on the throb in his head, he needed a break. Curious, he pulled the envelope closer. It felt like several photos had been printed. He sighed. “Probably pictures of Jackie’s flower bed. Didn’t appreciate my asking them to go through her equipment.” He tore open one end and let the photos slide onto the desk. These were larger than the paper copies, and much clearer.

He recognized three of the men currently residing in the morgue. He flipped to the next picture and frowned. The unclear person hovering in the background of the paper photo had been cropped and enlarged. Hayes? The man hanging out at the bar looked like Officer Hayes. Marshall dug through more of the photos. At least three included the newest officer to Dalton’s station. Once could be a coincidence. But three separate occasions? He checked for a time stamp, but that data hadn’t been included. The light was different. Clothes changed. Venue changed. The throb in his head turned to pain. He gathered the photos and slipped them back into the envelope.

“Brenda!” Marshall hollered. The younger woman stood at his doorway moments later.

“I ordered the new…” she blinked as she slid a gaze toward the captain’s nameplate in the window by the door. “The district council should approve you as interim chief later this week.”

He dragged his hand through his hair. Changing the office name hadn’t occurred to him. “Thank you.” He sighed. “Get me a copy of Officer Hayes’ file.”

“Are you giving him a commendation?” Brenda’s face brightened.

He tried to smile. “Can’t give out secrets. Get me

that file."

~

"Knock, knock," Kathryn hit her knuckles against the wood frame of the doorpost, then wasn't sure what to do with her hands so she tucked them in her jacket pockets.

"Hey," Marshall greeted. His face had a gray hue and his eyes seemed bleary.

"Rough day?"

He waved her in. "Close the door."

She did and then settled on a chair across from him.

His smile seemed more genuine. "It's a big desk or I'd take your hand. How are you doing?"

Instead of responding, she walked around the desk and pushed herself to sit on the desk close enough to take his hand. His warmth was what she needed.

He stood and wrapped her in his arms. Kathryn rested her head against his chest, put her arms around his waist. They stayed together a few moments. Kathryn could feel tension easing from them both.

He kissed the top of her head, returned to his seat, but continued to hold her hand. "Did you get any sleep?"

"Best night I've had in weeks. What's wrong? Other than the obvious. I'm so sorry about Captain—"

"It's not your fault." He interrupted her. "These came in yesterday." He tapped the large white envelope.

Kathryn pulled on one end and let the photos fall into her hand. She flipped through a few, then went back to the first. "Is that?"

"Makes Richard's response a lot easier to understand."

"What are you going to do? Where is he?"

"I've got to find more evidence. These could easily be explained."

"But you don't think he's innocent? Couldn't he have been killed by Richard's bullet?"

"The timeline fits. He's been here half a year. He's from Philadelphia. Explains why a gang of jewelry thieves were in our area. Small town, keeping things quiet until they could sell the merchandise. Someone helped take the heat off long enough for them to get out of Philly."

"But Hayes?" The man had an unremarkable face. She looked at more photos. He blended in the background. She tapped another of the men in a photo. "That's the man from the warehouse." She touched her cheek. "He hit me with his pistol."

"Him we know. John Lowden. His prints matched up in Europe and Canada. Interpol insisted on a live feed viewing of the body."

"How do we get Hayes?"

"I want to get a look at his file. There has to be something to connect him with the others. Until I've got something solid, I don't want him to suspect we're onto him."

"He's at rehab, isn't he?"

Marshall nodded. "Soon to be released. I expect he'll be able to resume work in a week or so. We need to find those jewels before he does."

"We were going to look for an artist studio." Kathryn shuddered.

He squeezed her hand. "Things got sidetracked. Can Lizzie tell us where it is?"

She shrugged. "JD said she's still out of it. Might be

a day or two."

"Then we search. Like you said before, there can't be too many in a small town like ours."

She squeezed his hand. "I'll do some research."

"I'll visit Hayes."

She started. "Is that wise?"

"Probably not. How else am I to gauge his part in this?"

Chapter 28

"Sarge," Hayes called with a wave. He grimaced, rubbing his shoulder. "Keep forgetting the rehab thing is just beginning to work."

Marshall schooled his features, squashing the urge to bump against Luke's wounded shoulder. He sat across the small round table. "Rehab agrees with you."

"I tried to convince my cadre of nurses to follow me here." He studied Marshall for a moment. "You look beat."

Marshall cracked a smile. "You should see the other guy."

Hayes leaned in. "What is going on? Seems like we've had nothing but death and mayhem the past month. I mean, Breyer? I can't believe it."

"Being short-staffed doesn't help."

Hayes tried to stand. "I'm ready."

Marshall motioned him to be seated. "When the doc says you're ready. Still got to find those jewels. An insurance company is putting pressure on solving the case."

"Do you know where they are?"

"We're eliminating possibilities. Unless they dug a hole in the middle of nowhere, we'll find them eventually."

"All five men from Philly are dead?"

Marshall nodded. "Means we'll never know what brought them to Florida."

"Let me talk to the doctor. I can at least help look for places, take a little of your load."

"You have to have a psych eval before I can reinstate you."

Hayes rolled his eyes. "I talked with someone in the hospital. I got shot, not unexpected in our line of work."

"Protocol. You know how much city council loves that word."

"Let's start working on them. The sooner I get my feet back on the street, the better."

He couldn't picture the young man as anything other than an eager, dedicated officer itching to get back to work. Marshall wasn't sure what to do with the doubts creeping in.

Hayes rolled his shoulder forward and then back. "Have they made arrangements for Breyer?"

"The family's all here now. I expect they'll make an announcement soon."

"Keep me in the loop."

Marshall smiled. "That's what Brenda's for, isn't it?"

Hayes' eyes shuttered. "She's a sweet gal."

Marshall had expected him to show more interest. He stood. "She's sweet on you. If you don't feel the same, let her down easy. I don't need my dispatcher in tears."

"Yes, boss."

"I'll see you later."

"Tell doc you've got some light work for me to do. No point wasting away in here."

"We'll see." Marshall turned away. Was Hayes a cold-hearted thief, possibly killer? Or did someone worked hard to make him look that way? Marshall sighed, stepping into the cool autumn sun. Now what?

~

Kathryn didn't need to ask how the visit went. Marshall's grim face showed he struggled. "I have the address of the place from the magazine. Let's head over there."

Marshall nodded. "Have you heard from JD yet?"

"No."

"Of course not. That might make our investigation smoother."

The Buick bounced over a pothole, causing Kathryn to giggle. Marshall gave her a dark glance. She protested. "You're the one talking about bumpy."

They arrived at the artist studio complex.

Marshall showed the pictures of Wes, James, and Alex to the woman at the receptionist desk. "Have you seen any of these men?"

Her brows rose. "Are these arrest photos?"

"Trust me, these are preferable to the other set I could show you."

She glowered. "These spaces are rented by artists. They have an expectation of privacy."

"Not if they break the law."

"Whose law?"

Kathryn could see a vein pulsing at Marshall's

temple and stepped in front of him, closer to the desk. "We're not here to invade anyone's creative space. We just want to know if you've seen any of these men. Or a woman who looks like me. She's my twin, and she's disappeared. I think she worked with one of these guys in a studio."

The woman shook her head. "I haven't seen any of them or someone who looks like you."

"Are there other places like this in town? From the article, it sounded like there could be several."

The woman glanced at Marshall, then pulled out a sheet of paper and wrote on it. "These are the other two I know. Sondy's is an old strip mall, but Alicia Vanoff has a converted Victorian in town. Close to Main Street."

"Thank you."

"I hope you find your sister."

Kathryn took a breath. "Me too."

~

Tammy Vanoff nodded. "Yeah. He has a studio." She tapped Wes' face. "Works with metals for jewelry. Started letting this other woman use the space too. He didn't think I would notice." She blew a small gum bubble and broke it. "I bet he'll notice the higher bill this month."

"Can we see his studio?"

"Do you have a warrant?"

"No."

"Then I'd say we're done here."

"An artist doesn't have an expectation of privacy."

"Their work is proprietary."

"Did you go to law school?"

"Even graduated." She blew another bubble.

"Discovered a higher purpose than practicing."

"Great. We'll be back."

"Oh, I love that one. Want to try it with a deeper, accented voice?"

Her teasing made Kathryn's lips twitch. She turned before Marshall could catch a glimpse.

"Smart aleck woman," he muttered, then punched speed dial on his phone. Brenda's name flashed. "Get me a warrant drafted for 227 Fletcher. Studio of Wesley Monroe or whatever alias he's used. The receptionist recognized him, so we know he has a place there."

Gaining the warrant took close to twenty-four hours. Tammy shook her head after narrowing her glare at Marshall. She handed Kathryn the key. "Enjoy."

"Which studio is it?"

She sat and ignored them, turning her attention to a thick novel. Marshall grunted and walked into the long hallway. It didn't take long for them to figure it out themselves. Midmorning sunlight lit the room. Tools lay scattered across the floor. Drawers were pulled from the desk, contents dumped. Seat cushions on a pair of chairs had been ripped apart.

Kathryn whistled. "Someone was looking for something."

Marshall righted a rectangular drawer lying on its side. "This is recent."

"Last night, recent? Or within a few days?"

"I don't see dust on stuff. Let's get the crime scene unit over here." Marshall stepped out of the studio to place the call.

Kathryn studied the contents tossed around the room. She faced Marshall when he returned. "Could Hayes know this location?"

"I saw him three days ago. He could barely lift his arm. How could he have known?"

They looked at each other across the mess, and then spoke the same name at the same time. "Brenda."

Marshall nodded reluctantly. "If he's who we think, his relationship to Brenda could gain him valuable information."

"How long have you known her?"

By Kathryn's tone, he knew what she thought. "Brenda will be devastated. She isn't helping him. I've known her since we started visiting Gram and Gramps in elementary school. She's close to Andy's age. Used to think they'd end up together."

"Andy?"

Marshall rubbed his neck. "Younger brother. He's out and about in the world somewhere. Not a hometown boy anymore."

"If you're certain you trust Brenda, we need to find her. What'll Hayes do when he has what he's looking for?"

"I still can't wrap my head around …"

"Work on the assumption that makes the most sense until new data changes our course. Do you think he found the jewels?"

Marshall didn't appreciate the tightening in his gut. He wanted to object to Kathryn's candor, but on what grounds? He searched the area. The corner cabinet overhead remained undisturbed.

"What?" Kathryn looked in the direction Marshall pointed. "He didn't finish searching."

"I doubt because he was disrupted. You were right. The jewels were here."

"Then the only one he's missing is what I picked up

from Callie."

"The collar's locked up at the station."

"Does Brenda have access to the property room?"

"She wouldn't go in there."

"Hayes would."

"He'd have to force her. We need to find Brenda now."

CSU hadn't arrived, but they couldn't afford to wait. They stopped at the receptionist desk. Marshall tapped the granite counter with the ring he wore on his pointer finger. "You better hope we don't find another key on our suspect. You could face charges if you let him into the studio."

Her smirk faded. "I didn't let no one back there."

"Where's the security video to prove it?"

"You'll have to take my word."

He shook his head. "Struggling with that. CSU will be here. The warrant's still valid." Light flashed across the wall behind the woman. Marshall turned to look. "Good. They're here."

"No," the woman's eyes glinted. "You're supposed to say it like they're here." She used a sing song tone reminiscent of the poltergeist movie.

Kathryn turned her head, but Marshall could feel her silent laugh. "Let's find Brenda." He frowned at the other woman. "Too much pop culture can't be healthy for you."

Chapter 29

"Brenda," Kathryn gasped at the sight of the young woman on the floor. Blood had dripped across her forehead.

Marshall ran to Brenda, crouching beside her to press his fingers against her neck.

Kathryn held her hand against her chest. "Is she?"

"She's alive," Marshall leaned back when Brenda moaned.

"I'll call a paramedic," Kathryn pulled her phone from her back pocket. She fumbled a moment trying to remember how to bring up numbers to dial. "Stupid phone. Don't know why they didn't have the same model that got smashed."

Brenda opened her eyes. "What happened?"

Marshall covered her with a sweater hanging on a nearby chair. "Don't know. Keep still. Looks like you have a knock on your head."

"That would explain the pain." She closed her eyes for a moment, then nearly jerked herself to a sitting position. "Hayes!"

Marshall pushed against her shoulder to keep her down. "Did Hayes hurt you?"

Kathryn tried to follow the conversation while she talked to an EMT. "No, she doesn't sound like she has slurred speech. Her head hurts when she moves."

"Hayes wouldn't hurt me." Brenda tried to touch her temple, but Marshall grabbed her hand.

He squeezed gently. "Who hit you?"

"I don't know. Hayes cried out to warn me, but I mustn't have moved fast enough."

"Did you unlock the evidence storeroom?"

Kathryn focused on her other conversation. "Yes, come check her out. Make sure she's okay. She may need stitches."

"Stitches?" Brenda's eyes widened. She reached for her head again.

Marshall frowned at Kathryn but held Brenda's hand.

Kathryn smiled. "Help's on the way."

"Did you unlock the evidence room?" Marshall asked again.

"Of course not." Brenda twisted her head to see behind her. "It's open."

"Do you keep a key in your desk?"

"The locked portion of my desk."

Kathryn moved to the dispatcher's desk. A blue purse lay on its side, the contents dumped around it. "They found your desk keys in your purse." The center drawer of the desk was open.

Marshall glanced at her. "Check the storeroom. We'll have to thoroughly photograph everything. Make sure some other case doesn't try to use this as a technicality."

The storeroom was further down the hall from Marshall's office. Keys dangled from the doorknob. "Maybe it's time to upgrade to electronic locks," Kathryn called.

"What?" Marshall's deep voice drifted from a distance.

Contents of the room seemed undisturbed. A single box placed on the table in the middle had its lid off. Someone knew what they were looking for, and they knew where to find it.

Marshall arrived in the doorway. "What did you find?"

Kathryn turned. "Don't leave Brenda on her own."

"I didn't. The cavalry arrived. She doesn't want to go to the hospital, but I told her they have to check for a concussion."

"Do you think Hayes hit her?"

"Brenda doesn't. He tried to warn her." Marshall rubbed his bristling chin.

Kathryn could hear the scrape of his coarse hair on his fingers. "Then what?" She ignored the tingling feel in her stomach. "They force him to open the door and steal the collar?" Kathryn looked at the table, and then the rest of the room. "Nothing else looks touched. How did he know where to find the right box?"

"He knows how to access file records."

"From his computer?"

Marshall nodded, and they both rushed from the room.

Kathryn stopped beside the gurney where a pale Brenda held an ice pack to the side of her head.

Brenda gave a soft grin. "I should be helping you."

"Getting knocked in the head makes that difficult," Kathryn smiled. "Hey, why were you and Hayes here? I thought he needed to stay in rehab another week."

"He called this morning and asked if I could give him a ride home. I shouldn't have, but I routed the switchboard to my phone. He wanted to drop in and grab some things from his desk. I know he's been itching to get back to work." Brenda closed her eyes.

"It's okay. You can explain later," Kathryn assured her.

"No, it's not that. He broke down when he saw the burn marks. You know… where the truck? I gave him some time alone. I heard him come in a few minutes later."

"Are you grilling her?" Marshall asked.

The EMT unlocked the wheels of the gurney and rolled Brenda toward the door. Kathryn moved closer to Marshall. "I asked what she and Hayes were doing here. It was his idea. Did you know they were releasing him from rehab this morning?"

"Doctor said the end of the week. It's only Tuesday. I checked his computer. The hard drive's been wiped. Tech might be able to recover something."

"They can at least use the network to see when he last logged in. What will Hayes do if he has all the jewels?"

"I'm not sure. I'll need to dig into his background. You're still recovering. Head home. Rest."

Kathryn laughed. "I'm not one to nap in the middle of the day."

"You could always work on your letter of resignation."

"Resignation from what?"

"Miami. I'm sure you can find a district further north in desperate need."

Kathryn wanted to protest. She liked Miami. Liked the challenge of working undercover.

~

He didn't like her silence. They made a good team, but she could probably say that about anyone she worked with. Like JD. Marshall cleared his throat. "I'll meet you for dinner. See if we have a plan for the next step by then."

Her hazel eyes met his and held for a moment. "Where do you want to meet."

"I'll pick you up."

She rolled her eyes. "I doubt there's anyone else to kidnap me."

"I wouldn't be surprised. I'm going to lock up the back and then I'll drop you off."

She sighed. "Or I could get my jeep out of the impound."

Marshall gave her a look. "Or you could get your jeep out of the impound. They'd probably appreciate that."

"Besides, you need to call an interim dispatcher."

"I'm still picking you up at your sister's house at six."

She saluted. "Aye-aye Captain."

Chapter 30

Kathryn stared uneasily at the front of the porch. Behind the drawn shades, a glimmer of light shone. She hadn't left a light on. The street appeared normal. The few familiar vehicles were in driveways or parked close to the curb. She clicked the safety off from the Sig Sauer and exited her jeep. The steps creaked as she climbed to the porch. No movement. Nothing disturbing the afternoon. She kept her hand against the butt of the gun and pushed the silver key into the door. The bolt slid smoothly, and she pushed the door open. A lamp on the hall table glowed, providing enough light to see into the living room where the shades had been drawn. Still, nothing stirred. She closed the door and drew her gun into the open. The floor behind her groaned. She turned, aiming.

"Kathryn." JD lowered his arm.

She held the Sig steady. What was he doing here? "Where's Lizzie?"

"Why are you pointing a gun at him?"

The sound of her sister's voice caused her to spin

again. She holstered her weapon. “What is going on?” Lizzie threw her arms around her without answering. For the moment, she didn’t mind. Kathryn hugged her sister.

~

“Marshall Franklin, stand still a moment and listen.” Jackie blocked the doorway into his office.

He faced her. “What?” He frowned when he realized who it was. “What are you doing here? How did you get here?”

She pursed her lips and stood with wrists on her ample hips. “You have to talk to him.”

“Richard?”

She nodded.

“I already did. You’re supposed to be in Tampa.”

“He’s not being honest. I’m his mother. I know when he’s lying.”

“I agreed to keep him here for his safety, but you aren’t supposed to be talking with him. He thinks you’re in danger.”

“But that’s just it. He’s begging that pitiful excuse for council to send him to the main facility. He’s the one who’s in danger.”

Marshall moved around the desk and turned a chair slightly toward Jackie. “Have a seat. What are you doing here? We left the three of you in Tampa yesterday. Where’s Lizzie? Does Kathryn know you’re here?”

Jackie sat in the leather-cushioned chair with a harrumph. “You have to talk to my boy. He won’t speak to me. I know he’s made mistakes. Big ones, but he doesn’t have to pay with his life, does he?” Her eyes filled with tears.

Marshall sat beside her, taking her hands in his. “I have no intention of letting him be sent to the county jail. How did you get here?”

“I insisted JD drop me off. I told him I’d walk if he didn’t.”

“Was Lizzie with you as well?”

“Of course, but she didn’t need to come here. She went home. At least, I think JD took her home. I told them Brenda could drop me off after I’ve seen Richie.” She held up a card Lizzie provided with an address.

“I’ll take you. We’re spread thin for the moment.”

“What of your young officer? Will he return soon?”

“Sooner than he planned, if I have my way.”

She opened her mouth. “Marshall Franklin, you let that man heal before you force him to work.”

“The physical therapist will clear him Friday.”

“I’m glad.”

“I know you are.” He gave her upper arm a gentle squeeze. “I’m sorry for what’s happened.”

“Some things in life can’t be anticipated or even dreamed. We do the best we can when we’re faced with the reality.”

Jackie shuffled away. Marshall reached for the phone. Faith, despite circumstance? Had he ever taken the time to know Jackie, or only formed his opinion of her based on the few seconds of interactions he’d experienced through the years? The dial tone chirped in his ear. He shook himself. Focus. He pressed Kathryn’s number. No response. Nabbing his keys, he headed out of the office. Late afternoon sun hovered in the west. The haze indicated a change in the weather closed in. He nodded at the officer entering the building. “Man operations. I’ll give a call if we need help.”

Jackie followed Marshall. He opened the door of the Buick for her.

~

Kathryn wrapped her hands around a warm mug of tea JD provided on a platter. She looked at her sister who seemed as pale as she'd been that morning. "What are you doing here?" She glared at JD. "She was barely conscious this morning."

He held up his hands. "Lizzie is every bit persistent as her sister."

"You left Jackie in the hotel alone?"

"No. She insisted returning with us. I dropped her at the station to see her son."

"We don't want her to see her son, that's why we took her to Tampa."

Lizzie shifted. "She sat with me hours every day. I think I heard the entire Pride and Prejudice novel." She grimaced, holding a hand against her belly.

Kathryn set her mug on the coffee table. "Your wound hurts. Should you be out of the hospital?"

"Doc said it's going to hurt. The infection is gone. That was the most threatening."

"What happened? How did you let yourself get shot? Why didn't you wait for me?"

"I didn't let myself get shot. Wes called. Said he needed to see me. He was sweet. Kind of sad, really, but he wouldn't hurt anyone."

"He shot you."

"Wes? He wasn't there. The other guy, I don't remember his name. We had dinner the week before. Supposed to be just Wes and me, but there were others. An entire gang."

Kathryn leaned closer. "How many?"

"Eight or nine of us, I think. Wes and me. John. He gave me the creeps. Wes said to go the other direction if I ever saw him." She shivered. "I'd be scared to turn my back to him."

"Who else went to dinner?"

Lizzie leaned back. "Does it matter?"

"It does. If you can remember."

She sighed. "John had a girl with him. The guy who showed up at the parking lot had a girl with him. There were a couple other guys who stayed quiet. One more at the other end of the table." She mimicked straightening the lapels of a jacket. "He looked different. Better dressed."

"Did you catch his name?"

Lizzie tilted her head to the right, thinking. "Luke something? Maybe?" She took a deep breath, pain flickering across her face. She leaned her head on the back of the couch and closed her eyes.

"That's enough with the questions." JD returned to the room. Kathryn raised a brow, but JD didn't back down. "She needs to rest."

"I'm still in the room," Lizzie interjected without opening her eyes.

Kathryn stood. "I need to talk with Marshall anyway."

Marshall spoke from behind them. "Just got here, actually." He glared at JD. "Want to explain why you brought them back?"

Kathryn waved her hands. "They aren't fugitives. I didn't know they were here until I got home."

"Your sister has a lot of questions to answer. Who knows how deep she's in this mess."

JD stood taller, stepping into Marshall's line of

sight to Lizzie. "She's resting."

"Wake her up."

Kathryn rolled her eyes. "JD, you do not have to stand guard. We are all on the same team." She glanced at Marshall. "All of us, including my sister. Kitchen. Now." Kathryn moved toward the kitchen without waiting to see if the men complied. If they were smart … she heard a footstep behind her. She sat on one of the stools at the island. Marshall joined her but remained standing. She looked at Marshall. "You have no reason to get huffy."

"Your friend is supposed to be watching over Jackie. Instead, she waltzes into the station alone."

"He thought the threat was over, so he came back here. Jackie insisted on seeing her son. Lizzie's in no shape to be walking around."

"Richard wants to be sent to the county jail. Do you know what they'll do to him? He shot a cop."

"A bad cop."

"We don't know, not for certain."

"Lizzie said Wes took her to a dinner. The whole gang was there apparently. She described a well-dressed young man on the far side of the table."

"You think she means Hayes?"

"The man's name was Luke. Coincidence?"

He sat on the stool beside her. "I don't like coincidence."

"Hayes seemed fond of Brenda. Maybe for real. He didn't want to kill her."

"I don't think he's killed anybody, but I can't keep hoping he's not involved." Marshall rubbed his hands over his face.

"If he has all the jewels, he's leaving town because

he knows he can't stay here."

"I'll send an all-points bulletin on his vehicle. We need to find out if he's affiliated with property in the area." He tucked a stray hair behind her ear.

Kathryn wanted to ignore the fact his touch made her heart beat faster. "You promised me dinner."

"So, I did. You can help me sort a pile of mail. Maybe the file from Philly will be in it."

"Order a pizza and have it delivered. Didn't you say that Palace place was good?"

"We're going out."

Kathryn stood. "Not if we're carting official police business with us. I want to see that file."

Marshall shook his head with a laugh. "Business first, just my luck. I'll get the box and call in the order."

Kathryn poured glasses of tea. The fact she knew Marshall liked his sweet … did she want to think about that? JD didn't like tea. There was nothing significant about him. Nothing significant about Marshall either. "Yeah," she talked to herself. "If you believe that, there's plenty of swamp land in Miami for sale."

"What?" Marshall asked, appearing next to her with a basket of mail.

"Nothing," she mumbled. "Did you get a pie with the works?"

"Of course. Even offered to share it with your boyfriend."

"JD will never be more than a friend."

Marshall dropped the basket on the island then pulled Kathryn closer. "Good to hear." He kissed her.

Too brief a kiss, but it didn't keep her heart from thudding in her chest. "You're not supposed to be more than a friend either." Her voice sounded husky.

“I think we’ve passed the just-friends stage.”

“Straight into complicate everything.” With a sigh, she stepped back. She picked up two letters on top of the pile of mail in the basket. “What are we looking for?”

“Someday, you’ll not be able to turn the conversation. For now, look for a return address with Philadelphia.” He took about half the pile and placed it in front of Kathryn, then searched through what remained. “Wait.” He pulled a yellow envelope. “Philadelphia.”

“Not very thick for a file.”

Marshall tore open the envelope and dumped its contents. They perused the file. Marshall turned a page then whacked his forehead. “Stupid.”

Kathryn looked at the page he held in his hand. “What?”

“The boat.”

“What boat?” Kathryn saw he held an evaluation with high marks.

“Not this. How could I be so stupid? Hayes took a trip last summer. Someone in the family owns a boat.”

“Where?”

“He posted a few Instagram images. We may be able to figure it out. Where’s your laptop?”

“In my bedroom. Give JD cash for the pizza while I grab the computer.”

~

Marshall felt the weight of recrimination. If memory served, the vessel looked seaworthy. Hayes could disappear. He pulled bills from his wallet.

JD jumped to his feet when Marshall returned to the living room. Dislike for the other man made him want to throw the money on the couch. Lizzie had been covered with a blanket. Her bare feet rested on a pillow. JD moved closer to her. His guardian stance relieved a knot within Marshall's chest. He managed a natural grin and handed the folded bills to JD. "We ordered pizza for dinner. There's enough to share when it gets here."

JD stood a moment then nodded. Kathryn turned the corner, lifting her laptop.

Marshall gestured toward the kitchen. "We're following a lead. Bring the pizza when it gets here." He turned to follow Kathryn, rubbing the back of his neck. He had no reason to feel relieved because JD cared about Lizzie. "God help me, I'm falling for Kathryn. Seriously falling," he muttered, watching Kathryn scoot onto a stool.

She opened her computer and punched buttons. "I've never used Instagram. You have an account?"

He moved beside her. The screen showed the Window insignia. "You'll have to download the app, then I can log in."

It took a few minutes, but they managed to scroll through the postings until they reached a selfie of Hayes standing on the starboard side of a boat. Kathryn tapped the screen. "He's still in a marina. There's a warehouse back there."

They searched more of the posts. Another photo showed the deck of a local restaurant. The sign dangling from the rafters had a picture of a sailboat with the name Dockies.

Marshall felt the familiar tingle of excitement. "This is what we need. Can't be too many of these around." He smiled.

Kathryn returned to the Google page. "Which coast do we search, Atlantic or Gulf side?"

"Gulf. He likes the lack of waves."

"It's in Clearwater." Kathryn called out success as JD brought two pizzas into the kitchen.

He looked at her screen. "What's in Clearwater?" He set the pizzas on the counter.

Marshall tapped his fist on the pale, marble counter. "Hayes has access to a boat moored down in Clearwater. It's about a three-hour drive. I'll be taking my pizza to go."

Kathryn stood. "We both will."

"Take a box with you," JD moved one box off the other. He opened cabinets until he found plates.

Kathryn closed her laptop. "I'll nab napkins for the car. I have a 4G adapter hookup. I can try to find the slip number while you drive." Kathryn got a grocery bag from under the sink. She added a wad of paper napkins then went to the fridge and pulled bottles of water.

Marshall opened the pizza lid. The smell of roasted vegetables and hot dough wafted over him. He grabbed a slice before closing the lid. Minutes later, with pizza stowed in the back seat, he held the door for Kathryn. She grinned, one hand holding her own half-eaten slice, the other with her computer and bag of drinks. Marshall took the packages.

She slid into the passenger seat. "I'll keep the laptop up here." She retrieved it from him and placed it on the floor by her feet.

He shut the door and jogged around to the driver's side.

Chapter 31

Even though night had settled long before they arrived, the marina had streetlamps and lights strung along the docks. Labels on the gates identified the slip they wanted.

"Boat's still there." Kathryn rubbed her hands together.

"Is Hayes? I don't see his vehicle."

She tapped his shoulder. "I've seen that car near the police station." She pointed at a silver Yaris.

Marshall felt like kicking himself again. "That's Brenda's. So much for assuming he'd switch to his own vehicle."

They climbed out of the Buick. Marshall searched the quiet rows of docks with their collection of ships bobbing as water rolled gently beneath them. Nothing moved. "He's got to be here. I don't want him to get past us." Marshall pushed the driver's door closed.

"I'm not."

The familiar sound of Hayes directly behind him

startled Marshall. He tried to swing around. Something struck his head and he fell into darkness.

~

"No!" Kathryn screamed when Marshall fell to the ground.

Hayes had his weapon trained on her before she could reach her own. "Don't."

"You're a cop. What are you thinking?"

"Keep your right hand up. Use your left to remove your gun and place it on the ground. Try anything, you're both dead."

Kathryn looked, but no one else shuffled around the marina this close to midnight. She motioned at the vehicle. "I'm not wearing it. Gun's in my purse."

"Place your hands on the hood of the SUV. I'm sure you're familiar with this drill." Hayes moved toward her.

She tensed. If he intended to do a proper pat down, she might get an opportunity to knock the gun from his hand.

He moved faster, grabbing and twisting her arm behind her as he pressed into a pressure point. Pain seared through her arm and she hissed. "Don't struggle," he warned. The grip didn't let up while he checked for a concealed weapon. Satisfied, he pushed her away. "Get your buddy on his feet. We're going on the boat."

It took them both to move Marshall. Kathryn knew almost nothing about boats. The watercraft looked sturdy. They stumbled up a ramp onto a main deck. A flight of stairs led down into the boat. Marshall remained unresponsive. Kathryn worried as she shifted, trying for a better grip around his waist. Hayes led them to a stateroom. They maneuvered through the doorway. Hayes released Marshall. Kathryn gasped, but Marshall's full weight unbalanced her, and they fell toward the bed. Hayes glanced up at the sound of footsteps on the deck. He kept the gun fixed on Marshall.

"What are you going to do?" Kathryn untangled herself to stand.

"You should have waited for morning. We'd have been gone, and you wouldn't have to worry about it."

"Who's helping you? The others are dead, aren't they?"

He didn't bother with a response. He walked out of the room and closed the door. She heard a click, and then the sound of two latches. They were locked in a room with a round window too small to climb through.

Kathryn sank to the floor, leaning against the bed. A hysterical urge to laugh lurked just below the surface. How did she manage to get locked in rooms by crazy men? Granted, Hayes waving around a gun didn't frighten her as much as her father. She pulled her legs up and rested her head on her knees.

She cared what happened to Marshall. Seeing him knocked down like that had pulled her heart into her throat. She tightened her arms to prevent her leg from shaking. *Miami is where I belong. I'm responsible for me, no one else—not my sister and not a man in my life.* She felt vibration in the floor. Hayes must have started the engine. *My best bet is to rely on me.*

"We can't rely on ourselves, baby girl." Memory of her mother's words came as lights in the room flickered. "Even when we think it's not good, he's making everything perfect."

"God's idea of perfect left you dead."

"God's idea of perfect gave me Heaven."

How many times over the years had she let arguments play in her mind? Kathryn shook the reflection and stood. The bed attached to a wood frame on the wall. There were empty cubbies and a couple of drawers. She crossed to check the doors on the other side of the room. The door on the right led into a closet. The other door opened into the bathroom. It was larger than she thought a boat would have. She turned the faucet knob, and water rushed into the sink bowl. She turned the water off. "At least we can use the bathroom." A loud moan from the other room reminded her to look for a towel. She soaked one end in water, then hurried to the bed.

~

"This doesn't make sense. What happened?" Marshall dabbed the towel where his scalp radiated with pain. Red stained the blue fabric.

"Here, let me." Kathryn pressed something against the wound. He wrapped his arms around her waist and rested his head against her abdomen. The vessel rocked beneath them.

"We're on a boat?" He pulled away.

"Yes. Good hunch. Too bad we didn't think to notify any locals."

"I can't believe I trusted him. We all did." He sank onto the galley bed.

"He had the perfect cover. Fund the heist, arrest the criminals, and take off with nearly one and a half million in jewels."

He cracked a smile. "And your family had to screw it all up."

"What can I say, I'm a lucky girl." She settled beside him, laying her head on his shoulder.

He pressed his face against her hair. She smelled of strawberries and sunshine. "You know, there's no one I'd rather have at my side right now."

"I don't know. I'm kind of wishing I'd stayed in Miami."

"And miss out on all this fun?"

"Oh yeah, I forgot about the fun." Her eyes met his, and the sarcastic façade drifted away.

The warmth of her eyes gave him courage. "You're worth it. Even if this ends as Hayes intends, meeting you has been my best life event."

Her gaze dropped. "What do you think he means to do?"

Marshall didn't let her lack of response discourage him. She still leaned against him. "Take us far enough out, he can dump us with no fear we can return to shore."

She chuckled. "Encouraging speech there."

"I know. Doom and gloom, but I'm glad you're with me."

"You heard what I said about Miami, right?"

"It isn't ending here. I've got too much to live for." He kissed her.

Her hand rested on his chest, and she pushed distance between them. "Let's find a way, then."

"Lord willing." He stood, keeping the towel against his head wound. The room didn't spin, so he felt encouraged. "Check the drawers. I'll shuffle through the closet." He crossed to the teak-finished door. The accordion slid open. A few shirts, slacks, a case on the floor. He heard drawers opening and shutting.

"Bathroom." Kathryn called, and her footsteps faded.

He stretched, pulling a box from the closet shelf. The shelf rocked. He dumped the worthless box of papers onto the floor and lifted the wooden board. He tossed it onto the bed. He pulled the suitcase next, but a small lock held the zippers together. He pulled a pair of pants from a hanger, snapped out the skinny bar, and used it to twist the lock apart. Men's underwear and socks along with a lady's nightgown were crumpled on the right side. He unzipped the cover to the left. Bingo. A cloth laundry bag jingled when he lifted it. Not dirty clothes. He couldn't resist digging his hand through the pile and lifting a palm of jewels.

"Wow." Kathryn joined him, running a finger across a shimmering emerald.

"Look. Here's your sister's design." He pulled a black dog collar from the bag. Silver studs had been patterned with sapphires."

"She's talented. These settings are perfect."

"We'll have to make sure you get the opportunity to tell her yourself. Find anything useful?"

"A flare kit underneath the sink. Has two flares, if they're still viable."

"I pulled the wood shelf. It's almost an inch thick."

Kathryn lifted it. "Sturdy. A decent hit could do some damage."

"That's what I hope. Did you notice how many they have on board?"

"Hayes helped carry you on board. I heard someone else but haven't seen them."

He shook his head and his stomach burned with acid. "So, at least two with real weapons."

Kathryn shrugged. “Options?”

Marshal picked up the board. “Let’s pray we get one down here and he has something useable against the other.”

They heard the floor creak from footsteps outside the stateroom. Marshall put his finger to his lips. Kathryn crossed to the side of the door that would open first. Marshall glared, but she mimed pulling someone into the room and him hitting with the board. Not a good idea, but the locks unhitched, and the knob turned. Kathryn ignored Marshall’s glare.

“You didn’t really think you could get the upper hand, did you?” Someone had grabbed Kathryn. She jerked back, her momentum pulling the stranger into the room.

“Not on her own.” Marshall swung the instant the man turned in his direction. The board cracked against the side of his head. Kathryn grabbed the sides of his jacket and helped him fall quietly.

“That was the fastest answer to prayer I’ve ever experienced.” Her eyes sparkled, and then she searched the stranger for a weapon. She held up a 9mm. “Somewhat better than a flare.”

“Check his ankles.” Marshall flipped the board over. Strong wood, not even a dent.

“Nothing.” She held the gun toward him. “You should take this.”

He shook his head. “I have the board. That’s your protection.”

“They’re more likely to come after me first. I’m the helpless woman.”

“Exactly why you should carry the gun.” He smiled. “Are we really arguing over this?”

"You? Yes, apparently you are, because you have about as much sense as God put into the board."

"Be that as it may, you're still carrying the gun."

"What do we do with him?" She nudged the unconscious stranger with her foot.

"Lock him in."

She looked around and pulled a shirt from the closet. She pulled his arms behind his back. "Hold his arms." She bound him, but it wouldn't take much to undo. "No handcuffs, huh?"

"I know. Not much use."

"Do you recognize him?" They both looked at the dark-skinned man sprawled on the bathroom floor.

"Never seen him. Where are the keys? We can lock the door on our way out."

After not finding anything else useful on the body, they found the keys hanging in the lock. Marshall twisted the bolt into place to secure the room and pocketed them. Gray carpet muffled their steps. Kathryn held the gun, poised for action. She allowed him to take the lead. He paused at the first door. He used a tight fist to signal stop. He listened. Nothing. A brief glance revealed the same. He moved forward until they reached the stairs.

Kathryn tapped his shoulder. She pointed to her eyes then up the stairs. She moved her thumb backward. He nodded. Something would be behind them when they climbed onto the main deck. He pointed at her and flattened his hand. She frowned. Of course, she wouldn't want to stay. He blinked. He could tell when she realized the plan. Her eyes cleared, and she offered a thumb up.

He climbed, gripping one end of the board with

both hands. Awkward, but if it prevented another strike to his skull …

"Drop it, Franklin." The click of a safety release followed the command.

Marshall raised his arms slowly and a shadow to his right grabbed the board. He took the last two steps to the top of the stairs.

"Clever, aren't you?"

He turned and faced his friend. The young man looked the same. His crisp white shirt worn open at the neck billowed in a slight breeze. Marshall glanced out the window. The boat skimmed across silvery waters. Moonlight reflected from the smooth surface. "Great night for the boat. Haven't been on for a while, have you?"

Hayes shrugged. "You keep me busy."

Another stranger remained standing at the window. The board leaned against the wall, out of his reach. The sitting area had three clusters of overstuffed chairs. Beyond this room was the pilot's control room. Or was it a captain?

"Where's Kathryn?"

He returned his attention to Hayes. There it was, steely eyes. He'd never noticed them before. "Your other baboon clobbered her before I got to him."

"And I'm supposed to believe that?"

A shot fired from the stairwell, and the man at the window fell backwards, crashing through glass. Hayes reached behind his back, but Marshall ran forward. Though the larger of the two, Marshall found himself defending his head from another blow. He elbowed Hayes' shoulder. The younger man groaned and bent over. With a growl of frustration, he leapt at Marshall.

Marshall spun, and the force sent them both to the floor. Hayes rose to his knees, weapon inches from Marshall's face.

"I wouldn't do that, if I were you." Kathryn stood a few steps below the top of the stairs, the 9mm held steady on Hayes.

Hayes looked from one to the other. "Do you know what we call this?"

"Nothing." Marshall kicked with his booted foot, connecting once more with Hayes' shoulder. A shot resounded through the cabin before he heard the gun thump on the carpet. Hayes writhed on the floor, cradling his arm. "Kathryn, grab his gun." He heard no movement. Looking over his shoulder, a shout of anger recourse through the room. He jumped to grab her before she fell to the lower level. Blood soaked the front of her shirt.

"No, no, no." He muttered, over and over, carrying her to the couch. Her wide blue eyes stared at him, drenched in fear and pain. He shoved Hayes down the stairs and locked the hatch. The other man hadn't moved. He raced back to Kathryn.

"Hold on there." He tore his shirt. Moving her arm, he lifted her shirt and pressed against her wound.

She gulped. Her face looked white against the crimson fabric of the couch. He wrapped her arms around her chest again. "Hold that. I've got to get this vessel turned around." He wiped her hair from her face. "Don't even think about dying on me. Got that?"

She nodded. He took that as a sign. With a press of his lips against her forehead, he rose to take control of the boat.

At least Hayes had good taste. The yacht responded

to the slightest touch. He turned her. He placed his smart phone beside the glittering console and opened the maps app. "Alright, satellites. Locate me now." In a matter of seconds, he zoomed out and oriented himself along the coast, using navigation to steer toward the marina. He called for the coast guard. All the while, he glanced back at the couch. Kathryn seemed to be holding her own. Her chest rose and fell. She started to cough. He slid the controls to autopilot and ran to her side. He lifted her, wiped blood from the side of her mouth. "Don't talk. We have to lean you up, keep you from choking on your blood." He placed several pillows beneath her head. "I'd stay and hold you myself, but someone has to drive the boat. Help's on the way." He ran to the control room. *Dear God, send help.* He aimed the boat toward St. Pete's. He almost fell to his knees when sirens screamed through the air. Rescue had arrived.

Chapter 32

Once again, Marshall paced the front lobby of a hospital. Kathryn had been air lifted to Tampa General and was already in surgery when he arrived. Security could glare all he wanted; Marshall refused to sit in the somber surgery waiting room. The other man with a gunshot wound had been brought to the same hospital. Hayes and the third kidnapper had been taken into custody by the FBI. He'd been blind. Hoodwinked by a twenty-six-year-old criminal in an officer's uniform. Richard's silence made sense. Jackie would be thrilled. At least someone would receive good news from these events.

He looked at the flat screen above the admittance desk. Stock prices rolled across the bottom of the screen. A reporter yammered about things that held no relevance to him. What if she died? He sank into one of the chairs lining the window, dropping his face into his hands. His heart cried out to God, but the jumble of words rolling through his head made no sense. A hand touched his shoulder, and he looked up. Jackie smiled down at him. He noticed others with her, Lizzie and JD. The three of them had come. He squared his shoulders, but Jackie kept him from rising.

"We're here for you, dear. She's in God's hands, and there isn't a better place for her. Come what may, we're in this together."

"I don't know what to say."

She patted his arm and took the seat beside him. "That's the thing about friends. You don't always have to have something to say."

"Not even to God. I can't seem to get words lined up to pray."

"God hears you, Marshall. He's heard you all along. God listens to your heart. You love that woman, and you aren't ready to give her up. He understands."

Lizzie said nothing, though red-rimmed eyes spoke of her hurt. Marshall stood, paced to the admitting desk once more.

~

"Told you I should have stayed in Miami."

Her eyes had barely opened, and she cracked a joke. Marshall swallowed the lump of emotion clogging his throat. "Hey there, Punk. You really look like it now. Your hair's sticking out in all sorts of directions."

"Way to make a girl feel special, Sarge." Her breath shuddered.

He looked at the monitors. Beeping continued.

"It's okay, I just feel like someone ripped open my chest and pulled out a few ribs."

He caressed her forehead. "Yeah, well. You're about right." Her eyes closed. "Stay strong. Hear me, Punk?"

"Eye-eye, Captain." She muttered, and then he could feel her body relax as she fell asleep.

Someone knocked on the edge of the door. He turned. A doctor waited. He took another glance at her before leaving.

"Husband?"

He shook his head. "Police Sergeant. That surgery took a while."

"The bullet made a mess. We had a lot to clean up."

"Did you recover the bullet?"

The doctor nodded. "Surgery station manager logged it in. Your forensic team can pick it up from there."

"How is she?"

"Lucky? The bullet ripped through the upper right of her lung and shattered two ribs. I'm amazed she didn't suffocate from air escaping into her chest cavity. It didn't hit her heart or the main arteries. She'll need time to recuperate."

"I'll make sure she gets it." He shook the doctor's hand and then he looked back at the bed. Luck? No, luck hadn't saved her. God was giving them a chance.

Chapter 33

Had he really thought God was giving them a chance? Weeks later, Marshall tugged the bottom desk drawer harder, until the old metal monolith gave way, and the stacks of files stored inside slipped over. He growled at the piece of paper drifting across his foot. The door creak open.

"What?" His tone brooked no patience.

"Uh, you're needed in the front, sir."

He straightened in his seat and glared at Brenda. "I'm busy right now."

"Dennis is out. No one else is around." She shrugged.

He sighed. He didn't mean to upset her. The world was off kilter, and he hadn't figured how to right it again. He frowned at the mess on the floor. It would still be there when he returned. Couldn't say the same about Kathryn. A week in the hospital and she left. Lizzie knew she meant to leave, but Marshall had been kept in the dark.

"All right. I'm sorry. I know we're short-staffed. Hopefully, we'll have a new officer on board in a few weeks." If he could get through the applications without comparing them all to a certain woman with long legs and short temper.

"It'll work out, you'll see." She smiled as though she read his thoughts.

He followed Brenda into the hallway, to the front of the station. Then his mind froze. Long legs, short temper, looking sassy and insecure stood in the lobby. "You're here." Stating the obvious, but his mind whirled with an onslaught of ideas. He wanted to kiss her. Throttle her. Send her back to Miami but hold her tight enough she could never get away.

"Yes. I'm back."

He stared, unable to say anything. Kathryn's smile wavered. He barely registered Brenda looking back and forth at the two of them. Brenda cleared her throat. "Why don't you take her to your office? Have some privacy. Looks like you need to talk about a few things."

"Yeah. Why don't we do that?" He motioned for her to slip through the swinging door. A light floral scent washed over him as she passed into the hallway. She didn't wear perfume before. He would have noticed.

She walked to his office. He followed her through the door, closing it behind him.

"I know it's been a while ..." she started to talk.

He placed his hands on her cheeks and pulled her close, his lips landing on hers. It was the best of his ideas. She filled his senses. Her arms wrapped around his waist. Need consumed him. He pulled away at the threat of losing control.

“Wow. Hi.” Her smile showed up easier.

“You came back.”

“Took longer than I thought.” She gazed past him, to a large portrait of an older man on the wall. “Is that …?”

Marshall turned to look. The formal sitting of Captain Breyer had been offset by the large photo from a company barbeque. With Kiss the Cook apron, one large glove, and a long spatula in the other hand, his mentor laughed at him every day. “Yes. That's Captain Breyer.”

She slipped her hands into her pockets and leaned against the desk, crossing her ankles.

“I went to see him.”

Marshall looked at the picture. “Captain Breyer?”

“No. My father. Paul Wainwright. I tried to visit him in Louisiana.”

“Why?”

“I told myself I needed to be sure they hadn't mixed him up with someone else. He's had a chip implant, so that can never happen again.”

“What was your real reason?”

She shook her head. “The only way he can stop having power over me is for me to forgive him. Forgive him for what he did to my mother twenty years ago, what he did to me now. He's sick. That’s all he's ever been. All he'll ever be is an old, sick man.”

“You think I should forgive him for Breyer?”

“No. Well,” the space between her brows wrinkled, “I mean, yes. That’s what we should do, isn't it? Not that I'm telling you to. And not that I don't have nightmares. But I'm trying.”

“Nightmares?” He stepped closer. The thought of

her alone in the dark, afraid, hurt him.

“A few.”

He pulled her into his arms, offering comfort. She fit against him.

“I thought you'd be angry with me.”

“I should be.” He looked down. She lifted her face toward him, and he brushed her hair away from her eyes. “I can't seem to feel that way toward you.”

She grinned, and her blue eyes sparkled. “I'm sure I'll do something by the end of the day.”

He laughed, giving her a hard squeeze before backing away. “I'm sure you will, Punk. Is that the only reason you returned?”

She sat down on the top of his desk, her long legs dangling. Not an image he’d forget. “I got to my apartment in Miami and realized it didn't feel like home. Never has.”

“And then you come here.”

“That's right. I felt closer to Lizzie than I have in years, though we’ve barely seen each other. While here, I worked with people I learned to care about. I became enamored with a community I want to protect.”

“Let's step back one. You work with people you care about?”

Her smile widened. “Of course. Brenda is delightful. Jackie is a dear. I still owe her a trip to the firing range. A few other officers grew on me.”

“Nobody else?” He slid forward a foot.

“Well, there's this one sergeant with the irritating habit of calling me Punk. I think he's jealous, because I have a larger gun than his.”

He stepped closer to her. “I think he's jealous because the world keeps trying to separate him from the woman he's falling in love with.”

“You shouldn’t end a sentence with with.”

“Why not, you just did.”

She sighed. “Just say you're in love with her, so she can say she's in love with you.”

He leaned close, a hair’s breadth away from her mouth. “I already did.”

“So did I.” She tugged, and he obliged.

Pounding on the door sometime later drew them apart. Brenda glared from the doorway.

Kathryn laughed, sliding from the desk. “I've got forms to fill if I'm going to complete my application.” She skipped from his office. Brenda tried to frown, but her eyes sparkled with mirth.

Laurie Boulden is Assistant Professor of Elementary Education at Warner University. She volunteers time with youth and ladies' ministries at Trinity Baptist Church. She is a member of Word Weavers International and has attended the Florida Christian Writers Conference five years. She has won awards multiple years in the novel category for Biblical fiction, fantasy and science fiction, and contemporary romance. She won Writer of the Year in 2016. She recently completed a Master of Art in Creative Writing and English. Her interests lie in writing as well as teaching others to write. A good story deserves a good telling.

www.ingramcontent.com/pod-product-compliance
Lightning Source LLC
Chambersburg PA
CBHW061021120726
47910CB00006B/2044

9781088167571